# Life in Translation

## A novel

## Anthony Ferner

Holland Park Press London

Published by Holland Park Press 2019

First Edition

A CIP catalogue record for this book is
available from The British Library.

ISBN 978-1-907320-84-2

Cover designed by Reactive Graphics

Printed and bound by
CPI Group (UK) Ltd, Croydon CR0 4YY

www.hollandparkpress.co.uk

The narrator looks back on the muddle of his life as a literary translator, moving between London and Lima, Paris and Madrid, Leiden and back to London.

He has long dreamt of finding literary fame, and has toiled away at his translation of an important but dauntingly bleak Peruvian novel. His is unable ever to complete the work, taking a series of dead-end jobs to make ends meet. For a while he earns a living at a large multinational company whose hidebound hierarchy infuriates him. At length he discovers his true niche as a translator of the works of a tricky doyen of Latin American fiction.

Over the years, friends, family, colleagues and lovers appear, disappear and reappear, but his edgy relationships with them seem to go nowhere. He comes to the painful realisation that he, a translator, is prone to 'misreadings': of his own strengths and weaknesses, of the women in his life, of his colleagues, of the viability of his translation career, of the options open to him.

The story is told through a mosaic of interlinked episodes that together create a picture of the narrator's bumpy road to maturity.

# Contents

# THE NIGHT OF THE UGLIES

The first thing that strikes you about Lima in winter is the greyness, everything muted under the low cloud layer. It's something to do with the city's location, trapped between the Andes and the cold Humboldt current. For a few short months there's a kind of summer. The first patches of blue appear in the sky around late November, and people's spirits rise. When I was there, back in the 1980s, I'd see the signs of the cloud lifting and the colour returning, and I'd go for long walks in the direction of the ocean as the morning mist burned off.

I was in Peru as a postgraduate student of literary translation at the Instituto Superior de Traducción e Interpretación, ISTI, or the Institute as we all called it. I've always been interested in languages. My father's job took the family to the Netherlands for several years. As a kid I learned Dutch by ear, and thought it was normal to speak two languages. I studied Spanish and French at university, and along the way picked up Portuguese and a smattering of Italian. I make sure people know I'm a translator, not an *interpreter*. Interpreters are the flashy ones at conferences or meetings of heads of state, who translate on the hoof: the adrenaline junkies, high-wire artists, prima donnas. The larger the auditorium the better they like it. Whereas the translators are the backroom boys and girls of the language world.

At the Institute, we were all ambitious and bright. The other students were Latin Americans mainly, but also Americans, Canadians, French, Spanish, and a few fellow Brits. We arrived at the tail-end of the Latin American literary 'boom': García Márquez, Vargas Llosa, Fuentes, Roa Bastos were all just about still writing.

I was besotted with Gabi, one of my fellow students. She was Peruvian, but her mother was English. She was small, a little plump, and ridiculously pretty. On the move

9

she was full of focused energy, always organising things and people. But in repose she had a languorous eroticism. I fantasised about her reclining naked in a Turkish bath, with kohl round her half-closed eyes, smoking a hookah and smelling of attar of roses. I imagined hips and belly and shoulders gyrating in syncopated rhythms. I'd have died of shame if she'd read my thoughts. She could be merry, but also determined and unsmiling. I found her a little intimidating, which only added to the enchantment.

When she was not busy with her translations, Gabi worked as a volunteer for the Peruvian Red Cross. In the February after I arrived in Lima, there was a police strike. Criminal gangs and the dispossessed of the city descended on the centre to loot stores while the police stood and watched, or shut themselves up in their barracks. The army came onto the streets, shot the looters and stormed the police barracks. Scores died. I remember the scary sound of gunfire after dark, and the clatter of helicopters directly over us day and night. The morning after the main riot, the road outside our flat was scored with tank tracks.

Gabi didn't like to talk about it, but her friends told me she'd been in the thick of the troubles. She'd had the phone call from her team leader, and she just got into her VW Beetle and drove up Avenida Arequipa to the centre. Wearing her bright blue Red Cross bib and hard hat, she stayed all day, carrying stretchers, tending to the wounded.

When things had quietened down, her Mexican friend Amparo showed me a copy of *La Crónica* newspaper with a grainy photograph of a Red Cross team in Avenida Emancipación. There was Gabi, kneeling over a man with gunshot wounds to apply a tourniquet; behind her an overturned car, smouldering. I keep the yellowed cutting in my South America scrapbook. At the time, I showed it to Gabi. 'Hey, Amparo tells me you're a heroine!' She just shrugged, went, '*Bua!*' and turned away. Her airy bravery was very attractive.

Gabi specialised in English-to-Spanish translation

10

– you always worked into your native tongue. As a result, she wasn't often in the same classroom as me at the Institute, so I was at least able to concentrate on the work, and avoid being distracted by her presence. When we did coincide in a tutorial, I'd gaze at her shiny black hair, or yearn to reach out and touch the curve of her neck where it met the exposed ear, and to finger the small gold stud in her perfectly formed lobe.

In coffee breaks and after classes we'd all sit around and argue about the art and craft and science of translation. We took it so seriously, obsessing over the latest theories, agonising about translation and power, colonialism and the appropriation of culture, the need to reclaim the source texts. We revelled in the difficulties of our task. Our battle cry was: 'Translation's theoretically impossible, let's do it!' And no doubt, at some level, it really was impossible, but we believed it to be essential all the same. A bit like life, as Gabi used to say.

Our tutors would set us to work translating short stories or fragments of obscure novels. One of my assignments was Benedetti's tale about love between two disfigured people, 'La noche de los feos', which would be rendered as something like 'The night of the ugly people', or 'Ugly people's night'. Gabi's friend Amparo had us all laughing by suggesting, with excessive literalness, 'The night of the uglies'. I settled on 'Night of the ugly', though nothing sounded quite right in English.

My translations from those days would probably embarrass me now. Technically they were just about adequate, but they always missed some subtle layer of meaning beneath the meaning, there was a lack of tradecraft, of cultural awareness. Take the simple word 'car', for example: *carro* in Peruvian Spanish. The word had a distinctive connotation in Peru, because young people lived with their parents, and the car, if they were lucky enough to have access to one, was where kids flirted, groped each other, had sex for the first time, often on cliff-top pull-ins overlooking the ocean, or in car parks late at night. How to convey all that in translating some coming-of-age novel into English, how to suggest all the winks and nods of the word?

When we weren't talking shop, we were eating, drinking and partying together, falling in love, breaking up, being happy-go-lucky or heartbroken in a frantic merry-go-round. I say 'we', but everybody else seemed to be more adept at this whirl of socialising, romance and lechery. I was making no progress with Gabi. I'd expected something to happen naturally, and when it didn't, I had no clue what to do next. The fear of failing paralysed me. I was the sort who worried too much about what could go wrong. Endless *what if*s.

At the Institute, a group of us would sit in the cafeteria and drink our mid-morning coffee. On one occasion, I was with Gabi and three or four other Peruvians. They asked me about Europe, which was a kind of Mecca for them, more so than Miami or New York. They dreamed of Madrid, Paris, London and Rome, of Copenhagen, Helsinki and Stockholm. At one point I mentioned the way young Danish women would cycle along smoking clay pipes. Gabi asked, straight-faced, 'And do they have beards, these Danish women?' The others smirked.

I said, 'No, Gabi, not on their faces.'

It took a moment to register and then they all laughed, including Gabi, and she mock-slapped me twice across the face going, '*Paf... paf.*' She said, 'Naughty boy, Chato!' *El Chato* was my nickname, roughly 'shorty'. I think that was the moment my infatuation became complete, but I still couldn't quite believe she was interested in me as a man rather than as a sparring partner in a group of friends.

Every few weeks, half a dozen of us would go out to a night club in Miraflores. The others would often end up fumbling together in the strobed darkness, but I was quite incapable of putting out my hand and touching Gabi. She seemed so in control, so assertive and sure of herself, it didn't occur to me that she might be waiting for me to make a move. Perhaps she was testing me, seeing if I was man enough to make a pass at her.

We sometimes went out to one of the crowded *peñas*, where live bands played the traditional coastal creole dances – the Spanish-influenced *marinera*, or the Peruvian waltz. The *marinera* was a sort of flirtatious, elegant courtship ritual with fluttering handkerchiefs and simmering eye contact. Gabi danced it fantastically well, with a sinuous sway of the hips. She once tried to teach me the moves but gave up because I couldn't get the rhythms. My ineptness was increased by her sweaty, sensual proximity.

Then at last something happened. The Institute threw a lunch for staff and students in honour of some national holiday or other. Tables were laid out under awnings on the lawn. There was a buffet of ceviche with sea bass and prawns, barbecued skewers of marinated beef heart, and much beer. The male students and the American and British women stood around drinking in little circles, each taking a swig from the bottle, passing it on until it was empty and then opening another. It grew dark and we moved on to spirits, downing *pisco saur* after *pisco saur*, each glass perfumed with the scent of passion fruit and lime juice, the rim frosted with sugar.

Gabi had quite a few drinks and became unusually jolly. She teased me about bearded Danish women. She made chin-stroking gestures, grinning at me from the far side of the lawn. As people began to drift away, she offered me a lift home. I hesitated, worrying about how many *pisco saurs* she'd put away. '*Ven, vamos!*' she laughed, and grabbed my arm. We got into her blue Beetle and were off. She kept driving onto the kerb at corners and I clung to the strap above the passenger door. She laughed when I screamed at her for jumping red lights. 'Come on,' she said in English, 'everyone runs red lights in Lima! If you don't, some jerk will rear-end you.' She smiled at me, and took her hand off the wheel to rub my thigh. '*Tranquilo,*

*Chato!'*

We parked outside my block of flats on Avenida Arenales, just before the tall office building on the other side of the road, the one with the big red neon sign for a Japanese electronics firm, 'National' I think it was. Paralysed by indecision, I stared ahead out of the window, trying to focus on the red neon. I was thinking how convenient it was that you could see the sign from such a long way off, so it was hard to lose your bearings making your way home late at night, when Gabi leaned across and started kissing me. I tasted that heady blend of alcohol and tobacco on her tongue, felt the soft touch of her fingers on my neck.

After a while, she pulled away.

I said, 'Hey, would you like to come in for... for a...'

She looked out at the lights burning in the ground-floor apartment. 'Your flatmate's at home?'

'Yes,' I said, 'Javier will be in. And Conrad.'

Javier was one of the Peruvians on the course, and Conrad a fellow Brit who was staying with us for a while, sleeping on a camp bed in the box room. He was a bit of a sponger but had a puckish charm, and excelled at the Peruvian *charango*, a small stringed instrument played by the indigenous Peruvians of the sierra. We called him *'El Demonio de los Andes'*, which was also the name of a brand of the local grape brandy, pisco.

Gabi pursed her lips, and tapped her fingers on the steering wheel.

I said, shivering, 'So, are you coming?'

'I'd love to, but I'll have to go home. I can't leave the car here even for five minutes, they'll tow it away. Or Sendero Luminoso will blow it up. Or I'll find it propped up on bricks with no wheels, and I'll have to go down to La Parada and buy them back.'

'That's a pity, I was –'

'You know what, Chato, it's late and I hate parking the car in the underground car park after dark on my own, it's so creepy, maybe you could, you know, come back with me, see I'm OK, it wouldn't be too far for you to walk…'

At some level, of course, I knew this was an invitation, but terror made me treat it at face value: a request to make sure she got back safely, and to find my own way home. I started to worry about that hike back to Avenida Arenales from her underground car park. It wasn't far, maybe twenty minutes at a brisk march, with the National sign to guide me, but there were vacant lots to negotiate, and cavernous potholes that could swallow a man, and there'd be some very dodgy people around after dark – Sendero Luminoso hit squads even – and packs of feral, possibly rabid, dogs.

But really I was scared of what would happen if I went back with her, of the possibility of failure. Would she have been sympathetic towards first-night nerves? Of course, we all have our insecurities. She might well have had her own; or not. I wasn't to find out.

I mumbled an excuse about having to get up at the crack of dawn. Javier and I had booked bus tickets to go into the hills above the cloud layer where we could walk in green fields and get some sun on our backs – true, but irrelevant. I remember the look she gave me, disbelieving, ironic, pitying. She touched her fingers to my cheek, said goodnight, waited for me to get out, drove off. I wanted to run after the car as it turned and disappeared from view, wanted to scream into the night, 'Hey, Gabi, come back, I'll go with you! I'll guide you safely home! Come back!' I was desperate to replay the scene, have another chance; my earlier fear already seemed ridiculous and incomprehensible. It was too late, of course. I stomped into the apartment and hurried to my bedroom.

I spent the night replaying our exchange in the car, my cowardice. I'd phone her as soon as possible to apologise. But what exactly would I apologise for? She hadn't said, literally, 'Come and spend the night with me.' What if I'd misunderstood, misinterpreted the cues? I went over the possibilities again and again, and at last drifted into a broken sleep.

Neither of us ever mentioned the incident, such as it was. She went down to Ica for a week, and I was busy with coursework, so we didn't bump into each other until sometime later. By then, it seemed inappropriate to apologise, and the significance of the events of that night had become vague and confused in my mind. I didn't know how to raise the issue, or to move on from it. I thought about simply asking her out, but she treated me with such friendly, collegial normality – teasing or serious, or distant, depending on her mood – that I felt the gap between friendship and something else was unbridgeable.

My hopes that, despite everything, something might still happen with Gabi were revived about two months later, when a group of us went on a trip to the wine-growing area of Lunahuaná, in the hills south of Lima. There were six of us squashed into Gabi's VW: Gabi, her mate Amparo, a rather haughty English girl called Julia whose London-accented Spanish made me cringe, Conrad with his armadillo-shell *charango*, Javier and me. We drove down the Pan-American Highway in the dark, a terrifying journey because oncoming drivers never dipped their main beams, and Gabi seemed to enjoy playing chicken with giant articulated trucks. We arrived late, found a dingy little guest house, and slept boys in one room, girls in another. After ten o'clock at night, the lights went out and the whole town was pitch black.

The next afternoon we visited the vineyard where they made *cachina*, a young wine that's used as a starter for *pisco*. It slips down like lemonade, and you forget it's alcoholic. The vineyard staff took us from cask to cask, ladling off glassfuls and handing them round for us to try. We got very merry very quickly, and bought several two-litre bottles to take away. After early dinner in a little restaurant, we went back to the guesthouse. We sat cross-legged on the beds, drinking *cachina* by candlelight and spouting off with mounting incoherence about power, domination and translation, all to the accompaniment of Conrad's plangent *charango*.

At some point I become aware that Amparo was leaning her head against my shoulder and nuzzling there. I felt uneasy, but was too drunk and lethargic to do anything about it. A little later she sat up and reached across to grab a green apple from a bowl on the little table. She took a bite, and offered the apple to me. I was just bringing it to my mouth when she cried out, 'Don't!' Everyone started laughing and shouting and pointing. A fat worm or maggot was rearing out of the bitten apple. I have an impression of it still, poking up towards the ceiling in the flickering candlelight, and wriggling, or rather undulating, like a tiny charmed cobra, casting tremulous shadows on the wall. As we watched, another worm appeared out of the core and joined the first in a swaying pas de deux; or perhaps it was us who were swaying.

Amparo shrieked, 'It's "The night of the uglies!"'

We all laughed. Amparo snuggled against me, rubbing my neck and whispering, '*Come-gusanos!*', worm-eater, so close to my ear it made me giggle. I noticed, even in my drunken state, that Gabi had fallen back against Conrad's narrow chest, and his arm was encircling her as if to take the bottle of *cachina* but in reality pressing up against her.

Time passed. Julia was rubbing Javier's neck and chest with her long fingers, her nails painted blood red. Objects loomed out of the dark, and turned out to be only shadows. Someone produced a joint and lit up, and the lazy curl of smoke filled the room. I became aware of an absence. I disengaged from a dozing Amparo and climbed over Javier, who was still entwined with Julia. In the corridor, I followed the high strummed notes of the *charango* coming from the other bedroom. When I pushed the door open, Gabi and Conrad were there, sitting on the bed with their backs to the wall, their shoulders touching. They fell silent as I entered, looking up with that bland, patient expression of people interrupted in intimacy. As

I left, the *charango* started up again, and I heard Conrad singing some Andean Quechua lament in his soulful voice. He knew I was besotted with Gabi. I think he did it for the challenge, did it because he could. I spent the rest of the trip hanging around with Amparo, increasingly miserable because I didn't feel anything much for her.

We left Lunahuaná on the Sunday night, later than planned, had a puncture on the Panamericana, and got back to Lima near dawn, subdued and tired. Gabi dropped me off a few blocks from Avenida Arenales. Conrad, in the front passenger seat, smirked at me, victorious, a little embarrassed, while Amparo gave me a sad, accusatory look; I'd let her down. Gabi just smiled, raised her hand in salute, and said, 'See you around, Chato.'

I walked to the flat in a drizzly dawn, angry with myself, unable to believe that I'd let another chance slip away. As I passed through a small square with a meagre patch of grass surrounded by low hedges, I saw a ragged man lying there in a torn overcoat and alpaca-wool hat, with a plastic bag of possessions. He was masturbating – avoiding eye contact, but undeterred by passers-by. *Lima la horrible.*

The next morning I set off early on a long circuitous walk to the ocean. As I turned into Avenida Salaverry, the cloud layer parted to show blue, and there was sun over Lima for the first time in months. At the end of Salaverry I crossed the road to the seawall. I climbed over onto the red rocks stretching out and glinting in the bright light. Dozens of little crabs were scuttling purposefully in and out of crevices. There was a faint breeze and I could smell the waft from the fishmeal factories. It was good to feel the fragile warmth of spring. I thought, *ay ay ay, compadre*, you're nothing but a miserable *come-gusanos*. I breathed in deep and bent to pick up a stone which I hurled seaward, straining to hear whether it hit rock or water.

I first met Julia Pinto Hughes in Lima in the mid-eighties, when we were both doing the postgraduate programme in literary translation at the Institute. My initial impression of her was that she spoke with a dreadful Spanish accent and had a superior attitude to the locals. She was plain Julia Pinto back then. The 'Hughes' she added later. It wasn't her married name, it was the matronymic she adopted as a second surname when she divorced her husband. Her closest friends in Lima were an American Marxist couple with whom she shared a grand, decrepit flat in the centre of town. The Americans – known to the rest of us as *los misioneros*, the missionaries – would go up to the slums on the bare beige hills around the city to help the inhabitants organise themselves and to demand basic facilities, such as a water supply; Julia merely talked the modish talk, as a lot of us did back then.

Julia had a forceful personality and great skill in cultivating ageing male academics. Apparently, she never lost the knack; many years later, when she had become an eminent professor, a colleague of hers in England murmured to me at a conference, 'But how could one ever refuse Julia Pinto Hughes!' There was always a combative side to her. Once or twice in Lima, I witnessed her slither, when thwarted, into molten anger that left fellow students quaking. Even the lecturers tended to indulge her demands ('How could you not give in to Julia Pinto,' as I might have said at the time).

The Peruvians found her intriguing, or rather the men did. They were fascinated by her straight blonde hair and the glimpse of white thigh beneath her leather miniskirts. They loved her aloofness, her disdain ('Who could be cooler than Julia?'). They even seemed mesmerised by her poor Spanish. Julia had a string of Peruvian suitors, mostly jaded married men, but also a few fellow-students, including my flatmate Javier.

I didn't have that much to do with her at first. I wanted to spend time with Peruvians rather than with other Brits. Sometimes, though, we coincided on trips or at parties. Her dancing was like her Spanish – lacking in flair and nuance, inattentive to the subtleties. Peruvian dances, whether from the coast or the Andes, are rather sedate and controlled, but she flung her limbs, gyrated her hips, wriggled her shoulders, looked moodily at the floor and pouted as she danced; too brazenly British.

I turned out to be pretty good at the dances of the Andes, which were easier to get the hang of than the more sophisticated Peruvian waltz that Gabi had failed to teach me. My unofficial tutor and dance partner was Marta Fuentes, a woman in her thirties who was married to one of the lecturers at the Institute. Marta was from the city of Ayacucho in the southern highlands, and when a song from her part of the world came on the record player, she'd make a beeline for me. The music has a lilting, limping quality to it that carries you along, especially after a clutch of *pisco saurs*. Marta had dark glistening eyes and short glossy hair swept up at the front. She and I became a dance item, almost a local attraction, encouraged by cries of *¡olé!* and *¡eso!* from the other party-goers that weren't entirely ironic. Unlike Julia, whom nobody could take for anything other than a *gringa*, I was sometimes mistaken for Peruvian on the basis of my authentic-looking dance moves. In hindsight, there was a spark between Marta and me, but at the time I was too distracted by my pursuit of Gabi to realise.

At one of those parties – it would have been a few weeks after my ill-fated trip to the hills with Gabi and the others – Julia turned up. She arrived late: *hora peruana* as they say, Peruvian time. As usual she attracted admiring glances from the men, suspicion from the women. She got herself a drink and came to sit next to me.

Julia was interested in a couple of minor female writers

at the end of the magical realism wave, and she aspired to translate one of them into English for her course assignment. I was snooty about her choice.

'Mónica Albacete? Really? She's so derivative. But then, you're a fan of Isabel Allende and the like, aren't you?'

'What,' she replied, 'are they not macho enough for you?'

'They're mediocre García Márquez imitators. And he only just gets away with all that tiresome magical realist stuff. I mean, come on—'

'I *love* magical realism,' she interrupted. 'That's what South America is all about. A parallel reality.'

'What, Lima? Magical realist?'

'Yes, yes! It really is.'

'Have you been dropping acid with the Americans again?'

'God, you're such a cynic. Anyway, they don't do drugs.'

'I'm not a cynic, I'm a romantic. It's just that I've had my fill of heroines weeping bitter tears till they flood the house, and ancestors with meaningfully symbolic green hair. I mean, give me a break.'

'And I've had my fill of over-inflated male egos like Vargas Llosa or Carlos Effing Fuentes and their hyper-masculine perspectives.'

'This isn't about gender politics, Julia. There are fantastic women writers who haven't been translated yet, so why—'

'Such as?'

'... So why aren't you working on them rather than on a gushy mediocrity like Albacete?'

'*Such as?*' she repeated. 'Name one.'

'OK, such as Beatriz Salgado. Her books are set in Lima, and they're powerful, epic, emotional. Or with your Portuguese you could be translating someone like Alma Sertão. Her work has incredible emotional resonance and

21

depth, and she wouldn't touch magical realism with a bargepole.'

Julia said, 'Alma *who*?'

I wasn't sure if she was joking or not.

'You've read so much more than me,' she said.

At the Institute they urged us to take in all styles and genres: 'Read, read, read. Read till your eyes bleed!' Not just highbrow fiction, but detective stories, popular romance, station bookstall thrillers. They told us to be alert always to tone and style, to vocabulary range and register. To ask ourselves continually: how would you go about translating that? What strategies would you use? How far do you have to be unfaithful to the literal text in order to retain fidelity to its spirit?

'Anyway,' Julia said, 'why are we talking shop?'

'I don't know.'

She got up and went over to the drinks table. I wandered through to the kitchen and helped myself to a bowl of chilli and chicken.

The party had filled and livened, people were stoked up on beer and *pisco*, a record player had appeared. The sounds of Andean flute, *charango* and saxophone floated through the apartment, plates were cleared and the dancing got going. Marta Fuentes came over, took my hand and led me onto the dance floor. We got into the swing of it, our moves second nature by this time, and the Peruvians began to call out their good-natured encouragements.

As we swung round, I noticed Julia watching us from the edge of the room. She seemed in two minds: scornful of me as a Brit trying to go native, as she saw it; yet envious of the attention I was getting.

Marta and I took a break. She went off to keep an eye on her husband, whom she suspected of having an affair with one of his students (quite possibly Julia). I'd barely caught my breath when Julia approached me.

'Good dancing!' she said.

'Thanks.'

'Well, more a kind of hoedown than a real dance,' she added. 'But you seem to have more or less got the hang of it.'

'I'm not much good really: "The wonder is not that it's done well but that it's done at all." That sort of thing.'

'Too modest,' she said. 'Want a beer?' I nodded. She handed me one of the two bottles she'd been holding by the necks, and took a swig from hers.

'You been having lessons?'

'No. Must be a natural.'

'Ha.' She took another slug of beer. 'That woman...'

'Marta Fuentes?'

'If that's her name. Isn't she married to Pedro Luis?'

'Yeah.'

'OK,' she said. She looked at me with her calculating eyes. I noticed she had loads of eyeliner on, but they still seemed too small. 'You screwing her?'

'Sorry?'

'Marta and you? You got a thing going?'

'What!' I said, as though the idea was ridiculous, though I'd certainly considered it.

She laughed and poked me in the chest, playful, one hand on jutting hip. I was confused. Julia had never shown any interest in me before, and now she appeared to be coming on to me. She said, with head cocked, 'You sure you're not screwing her?'

'No! I mean, *yes*, I'm sure. What kind of question is that, and from a feminist? Anyway, she's married, isn't she.'

'So?'

'We're not all like you, Julia.'

She chuckled, and said, 'Cheers!', clinked her beer bottle against mine. We both drank.

She looked at me, and stroked my cheek with her hand. *'Ay, inglesito,'* she said, or rather, *'Eye, inn-glay-see-toe,'* in her incorrigible, take-no-prisoners home-counties accent. *Oh, poor little English guy.*

23

Without warning, she became businesslike and earnest. 'So tell me. What are you doing for your translation assignment?'

'I thought we weren't talking shop.'

'No, go on, tell me.'

'It's not that interesting.'

'Come on, Christ! Just spit it out.'

'Well I'm doing one of Benedetti's short stories. *Night of the Ugly.*'

'Oh.'

'And you?'

'They've given me an absolute pig of a short story by Roberto Tunsch. *Enigma oscuro*, or something. I absolutely don't get Roberto Tunsch. Can't understand the Spanish, let alone translate it. He's Uruguayan or something, so...'

'Paraguayan.'

She sat down and patted the chair beside her. Obediently, I joined her.

'He's not so difficult,' I said, trying to regain the initiative.

'No?'

'Not really. Not once you enter the logic of his world. The fantastical emerges out of the banal and the everyday, so you can't see the join, and there's all this nameless stuff going on just under the surface, and... He's one of my favourite authors in fact.'

She was looking at me, biting her lip, eyes narrowed. Then she leaned forwards and put her hand on my arm. 'You can do it for me if you like.'

'What, your assignment?'

'Uh-huh.'

'Thanks, that's big of you.'

She shifted on her chair, frowning. 'No, seriously.'

'You've got to be joking, Julia.'

'No, I... if I knock out a rough version, would you have a look at it for me? Please? Just so I don't embarrass myself.'

24

I blew out my breath. I'd been backed into a corner, and knew that if I said yes I'd end up doing such a thorough editing job on her version that I might as well translate the whole story from scratch.

'Please?' She'd put on a little-girl voice and her hands were together in supplication.

'OK, I guess,' I said at length.

'Thank you!' She leaned across, put her arms around me, and kissed my cheek.

'Maybe you could also give mine the once-over?' I said, to save face as much as anything.

She giggled. *'I'll look at yours if you look at mine!'*

I blushed.

'I will, of course,' she said. She pulled a face. 'Not that there's much point, yours will be better than the original, knowing you.' I think she realised that the course was too much for her, that she was out of her depth.

I went for another beer and when I came back, Julia was talking to the director of the diploma course. OK, that's that, I thought: he'll be far more interesting quarry for her now she's got what she wants out of me.

I sat drinking by myself, wondering where Marta had got to. One of the Peruvian students, who'd just come back from the UK with a handful of disco albums and EPs, put 'All night long' on the record player. Moments later, Julia was grabbing my hand. 'Come on!' she said, 'can't sit down for Lionel Richie!'

I let her pull me to my feet and guide me through the throng.

We danced close and slow, our bodies sweaty and hot, alongside other couples in their own tight worlds. We were all tired, more than a bit drunk, libidinous; the fag-end of the party. Julia, her lips close to my ear, was singing along to the words. I felt the little puffs of her breath:

*Everybody sing, everybody dance*
*Lose yourself in wild romance, we going to*

The music stopped. There was a glimmer of light through the east-facing windows. She clung to me and said, 'Come on. Walk me home.'

I thought, what's this about, Julia, you've already got what you want from me. And as if in answer, she said, 'I'm feeling *so* homesick. Must be the music. After all those fucking tinkly-tonk Andean dances. Don't you ever get like that? I mean, don't you miss things back home? Like actual green grass for fuck's sake. I miss English voices, English faces. Proper music. Bowie.'

She began to sing, not taking her eyes off me. She was bobbing her head and shaking her shoulders to a beat in her mind. *Put on your red shoes and dance the blues, Let's dance, To the song they're playin' on the radio...* She broke off to say, 'Fuck I do miss Bowie.'

'I know what you mean,' I said. I wasn't feeling homesick, didn't care much for Bowie, adored all those fucking Andean dances. But the way she moved her shoulders was so eye-catching I wanted to wrap my limbs round her and dance close again, our bellies touching. I imagined us sensing each other's warmth through our clothes, the desire mounting. She reached out a hand and rubbed my chest with her knuckles. I felt a tremor of excitement.

'Shall we?' she said.

We stumbled out into the grey dawn and wandered through the quiet streets towards her flat. She'd put her arm through mine. She sang softly, *If you say run, I'll run with you, And if you say hide, We'll hide...* and at a street corner she stopped me and we kissed. My head was fuzzy. I thought, You're going home with Julia Pinto, what the *hell*, and I grinned to myself in disbelief.

We were two or three blocks from her house when it began.

The first thing was a dull rumble. I caught myself

thinking, *Oh, it's the 6:04 to Selly Oak.* Back in Birmingham,

I'd shared a student house on a railway embankment. I had one of those flat digital bedside clocks with red LED numbers, and every morning at 6:04 the first train of the day clanked along the cutting, making the whole house vibrate. *You're not in Birmingham,* I told myself through my alcoholic muzziness.

'Oh my fucking God,' screamed Julia, 'the ground!'

The sensation was eerie: the pavement beneath our feet, something that was supposed to be solid and fixed, was now wobbling around like one of those platforms on springs in children's playgrounds.

I stared, hypnotised, as across the street a building vibrated so violently that the bricks seemed on the point of jiggling themselves apart.

Julia was saying, 'Christ, is this an earthquake? Jesus Christ, we're in an earthquake!'

The movement grew stronger, with jolts, and pitching like the deck of a ship on a rough sea, and all the time there was a rumbling roar.

A rip appeared in the asphalt of the road.

To our right, masonry crashed down from the façade of a building and smashed into fragments on the pavement.

People were running out into the road, screaming, wild-eyed, dodging the early morning traffic. Mothers dragged sleepy kids, not knowing which way to turn. The blare of car horns became one long cacophonous blast.

I grabbed Julia and pulled her into a doorway with a solid-looking stone arch above it, the entrance to a bank. Others joined us, the men unheeding of women and children, jostling for the best spots. We held onto the walls and each other, suffering bouts of what I suppose you'd call land-sickness with every lurch and tremor.

The quaking subsided. I learned later that the event had lasted only ninety seconds, but it was just as people say: as though time had slowed, as though every moment

27

had been stretched to breaking point and made vivid with terror.

When the world's shaking stopped, my own began. I thrust my hands in my pockets to still them. I looked around. Relieved mothers crossed themselves. Frightened children began to cry, inconsolably.

I was thinking about how to get home through the chaos of hysterical people and piles of rubble when an aftershock brought more screams, another shower of masonry. People who'd started to edge forward into the street shrank back to the shelter of the entrance.

And Julia was no longer there. That was the last I saw of her in Peru. The next day I went round to her flat. The Americans explained that she'd already left for England, and was possibly going to enrol in a translators' course somewhere in Europe. A location, I supposed, where the food would be less spicy, the dancing less Andean, and the risk of earthquakes significantly lower.

My last recollection of Julia that early morning in Lima was of her clinging to me, her long red-painted nails engraving pink arcs in my forearm. I remember turning round and seeing her gone, and feeling concern for her, but above all cheated of my moment, dismayed at all the eager sexual anticipation thwarted. I wondered if she felt the same, whether she too had been left with that dull pressure in the loins.

Later, though, I told myself I'd dodged a bullet. I'd avoided getting entangled with a woman I didn't really like; didn't like because she was pushy, shallow and, when it came down to it, not much of a translator. The lust had been momentary, alcohol-fuelled. My one lingering regret was that I'd not had the chance to pit my wits against the sinewy elusiveness of Roberto Tunsch's *Enigma oscuro*; but maybe I could choose it for my next class assignment.

MACHINE TRANSLATION

In the mid-1990s, I lived in Paris for a couple of years, escaping an unravelling relationship in London. I found work in the translation department of a large American multinational, Electronica Inc, within spitting distance of the church of la Madeleine: I still wanted to be a literary translator, but I needed a day job to survive. They shoved me in a windowless broom cupboard of an office, with an old computer and a noisy printer for company.

My boss was a man of around fifty called Claude Boutonnet. We translators were known collectively as 'Language Resources', and were part of the 'Miscellaneous Services' which Boutonnet managed. He had a thin face, trimmed moustache, eyes ever on the verge of widening into a glare, and tense, gesticulating fingers that always seemed to be pointing at something in denunciation. He came to work on a racing bike, dressed in tight-fitting Lycra. Even in casual conversation, he had a harsh, barking voice. I found it alarming in the way that sudden loud noises are alarming. While he ruled over his underlings with a certain brittle authority, he was servile to those above him. His boss, the director of Administrative Services of which we were a far-flung dependency, was an affably vicious bully named Michel Chrétien. Boutonnet was terrified of him.

So, brutalised Boutonnet brutalised us in turn. He demanded unreasonable things of us, hectored us, interfered with the details of our work. If you interrupted his flow with a question or comment, he would plough on regardless. Or else he'd wait for you to stop, as if absent, or ostentatiously not listening, and when you paused, he'd take up his flow again as if you hadn't spoken. He spent a lot of energy just to maintain his authority over us.

Boutonnet had a habit of shrugging his arms down inside the sleeves of his navy-blue blazer while twisting his wrists, as if to ensure that a regulation military inch of white shirt cuff showed. At the same time, he'd make an oblique ducking movement of his head. I was a captive audience for his soliloquies. Perhaps because I was foreign, he treated me as a species of low-status confidant. I guess he didn't have that many people he could talk to. I know he had a wife, whom he always referred to as 'Madame Boutonnet'. I assumed this was to protect such intimate details as her given name from exposure to his juniors. He'd wander into my office, and glance around it with distaste, as if its condition was a moral failing on my part. He and I always spoke French together, though English was the official language of European Headquarters. The truth was that his English was poor.

Following a reprimand from big boss Chrétien for some minor error of protocol, Boutonnet insisted on signing off all translations personally before they went out. The predictable outcome was that he became a bottleneck disrupting the flow of work, sometimes for weeks. Chrétien's exasperation grew. After one meeting with his boss at which, rumour had it, fists were pounded on desks and voices raised in anger, Boutonnet slunk into my fluorescent-lit cubby-hole, sat down in a spare chair and said, '*Eh bien, Monsieur l'Anglais*' – which is what he always called me, though I think he did know my name – 'Monsieur Chrétien believes the future lies in machine translation.'

I looked at him open-mouthed. As if excusing himself, he went on, '*Ah, vous savez, Monsieur Chrétien, c'est une force de la nature!*' It was his way of saying there was no possibility of challenging this edict. 'I would like you as a matter of urgency,' he added, 'to draw up a report for implementing machine translation in Electronica.'

'Machine translation could only be proposed by someone who does not understand how translation works,' I replied.

At this *lèse-majesté* Boutonnet gave me an eye-popping stare. '*Expliquez-vous!*'

I always had the sense that panic lurked beneath his browbeating manner. 'People think what we do is like the work of glorified copy typists,' I said, 'just taking text in one language and churning it out in another. They think a computer programme could do it just as well, and quicker and cheaper.'

'And why not? Why cannot a computer programme do it?'

Boutonnet had the power to make my life difficult, and I needed the money. Still, I would not be totally submissive and he had riled me with his tone. I said, 'A computer programme cannot translate. People who don't know about language assume it's a matter of having two lists of words, one being all the words used in the source text – a novel, let's say, or a company report – and the other being the equivalents of these words in the language into which the novel's being translated—'

'Yes, yes, let's get to the point.'

'The point is, people think you simply enter both lists into the computer and press a button, and, *ô miracle*, there's your translation.'

'Computers are ever more powerful, I don't see what the problem could be.'

I said, 'Words rarely have simple meanings, and often their meanings are defined by their context.'

He was shaking his head and tutting, getting ready no doubt to sweep away my objections. I pressed on. 'Let's say we're translating something from English to French. The word "run" occurs in the original. How do we translate that? People will say, "Oh even I know that from my schoolboy French – *courir*." Well, yes, maybe. But what about "run over" or "run through"—'

'Good, OK, we can conclude this discussion, I think…'

'… So how do you train a computer programme, first, to recognise a phrasal verb and second, to know what the phrasal verb means in its context? For example: "I *ran over* the argument with my colleagues." Or "I *ran over* to

31

help my colleagues." Or "I *ran over* my colleagues in my Citroen 2CV."'

I sensed he did not understand the nuances of the English phrases. He said, 'Yes, naturally. These are details. There are always details. But if we allowed them to thwart us, we would never advance. They can be resolved later.'

'Or take the phrase "I *ran up* a large bill",' I continued. 'How would the computer know whether I'd incurred a massive debt, or had climbed the beak of some giant bird, or—'

He brought his hands together decisively and rubbed them. *'Bon, ben, ça suffit.* That will do. Please work on this as a matter of urgency. We need to see the big picture. Monsieur Chrétien requires a response by the end of the month.'

'Machine translation will not work, I can guarantee.'

'Nevertheless,' said Boutonnet, his hands flat on the desk as he leant forward, 'you will do it, *monsieur.*'

I said nothing. I probably sighed.

'Of course,' he added, in a more conciliatory tone, 'in every organisation, there is the *aspect galon*, the hierarchy side of things. Chrétien has more braid on his sleeve, more stars on his collar. *Vous comprenez?* We will see how things go. But one must assume that the top men have superior ability and that therefore one must evaluate their characters and get their measure before attempting to manipulate them.'

The idea of him manipulating Chrétien was laughable. Perhaps he really believed that was what he was going to do, perhaps that was what allowed him to live with himself, with his own servility. He leaned far back in his chair, tilting towards the wall, his hands behind his head: Boutonnet unbuttoned.

'If we do not play it carefully with Monsieur Chrétien,' he mused, 'Bildt will gain traction.'

Bildt, a Swede, was Boutonnet's great rival, though I don't think Bildt was aware of this. He worked in a different group within the division and had an easy jocular relationship with Chrétien.

Boutonnet stared at the ceiling, his hands still supporting the back of his head. 'A strange beast, Bildt. One senses a lack of respect, a lack of discipline. I speculate that he somehow evaded National Service; perhaps they do not have it in Sweden.'

I braced myself. When Boutonnet was in these ruminatory moods, the conversation, or rather the monologue, could meander in unexpected directions. My role was to listen in silence and nod frequently. Staring out of the window, Boutonnet continued and, by what leap of logic I'm unsure (though possibly it was because of Bildt's reputation as a ladies' man), he said, '*Les grands ne forniquent pas. Ils conservent leur forces, ils n'éjaculent pas.*' I nodded as required, uneasy at this disturbing glimpse into Boutonnet's psyche, but it was as if he'd forgotten I was there.

At length he swung his tilted chair back to firm ground and thrust his chin towards me. 'So, *Monsieur l'Anglais*, are we clear? Machine translation. Your finished report. On my desk.' He looked at his watch. 'No later than noon on the 25th.'

He stood up, gathered his briefcase and left my office. I sat there, thinking about handing in my notice. I'd imagined when I'd first come to work in the company that I would be able to play it cool, keep an ironic eyebrow half-raised, see myself as a kind of anthropologist investigating the culture of a strange tribe, and devote my energies to my literary translation. But I'd been sucked into this world, fallen subject to Electronica's arcane power struggles and esoteric conventions, and had been slotted into the hierarchy at its very base. Only cleaners and janitors were more lowly.

I went home, fed up with the idiocy of it all, the way people kept on doing stupid things because corporate logic and hierarchy compelled them to. Yet here I was, in the

33

same bind, about to do something I knew to be stupid. I decided I couldn't resign: I had no other source of income and wasn't prepared to go back to London with my tail between my legs, and memories of my ex, Rachel, still too sour.

I slumped on the bed, my small problem slowly pumping itself up into an existential crisis. Nearly a decade on from my time in Lima, I still felt unsettled: geographically displaced, emotionally dissatisfied. I thought in terms of 'Before Peru' and 'After Peru', my life neatly divided by the vividness of that experience. And 'After Peru' felt grey, the psychic equivalent of some soulless Eastern Bloc capital – particularly now that I was caught up in the coils of the corporate monolith.

I forced myself to get up off the bed. After a strong coffee, I went for a long walk to burn off the nervous energy. At first I feared I'd end up bashing my skull in frustration against the elegant Art Deco ironwork of some metro station entrance. But the walking changed my mood, and as I swung round at Île de la Cité to head for home, a plan of action was forming in my mind.

The next morning, having slept on it, I'd figured out the details. I would prove to Boutonnet that machine translation was unworkable. When I got to the office I opened Netscape and browsed the internet until I found a dull article on the health of the Spanish economy. I cut and pasted a paragraph into one of the new online translation programmes: Babelfish or some such. In a few seconds it had produced its response, garbage so ridiculous even Boutonnet would have to admit a computer couldn't solve our problems. The clincher was that it translated the Spanish phrase meaning 'peaks and troughs' of economic activity – *picos y bajos* – as 'pricks and bottoms'. I gave a yelp of triumph loud enough for the departmental secretary to come scurrying out of her office with a concerned look.

'Monsieur,' she said, 'is something the matter?'

'No,' I replied, 'everything is just fine.'

I apologised for disturbing her, printed out the page and went to see Boutonnet.

'Here is the demonstration,' I said, waving the paper. 'Machine translation is completely useless for our purposes.'

He read through the English, his fists to his temples. I glanced round his office: the reproductions of Chardin still-lives on the walls; the glass-topped coffee table covered in pristine editions of *L'Expansion* and *Newsweek*; the hatstand with the managerial coat and scarf; the knee-length Lycra bodysuit in purple and black, draped Dali-esque over one arm of the stand; the pointy cycling helmet dangling from its strap; Boutonnet's racing bicycle propped against the wall. Out of the office window I could see the blind wall of a warehouse or depository across the narrow street.

I was just musing that my boss must arrive at work hot and sweaty, come up in the lift with his bicycle, shower somewhere, and change into his business suit and tie, when Boutonnet tutted to himself and shook his head. He looked up. '*Eh bien*, we have a translation into English. That is sufficient, no?'

'But it's nonsense!' I pointed to the piece of paper: '"Pricks and bottoms"!'

He looked at me blankly, so I translated into French: '"*Les bites et les culs.*"'

Boutonnet blushed scarlet, handed back the sheet of paper. '*Bien*. That will do!'

'But—'

'Enough! I will hear no more objections or complaints. The report, monsieur. I want a rough draft. By Monday, if possible. Yes, by Monday. Midday.'

I went home to my cramped little studio flat, too dispirited to sit down and write my draft report, or even to work on the Peruvian prison novel that I was trying to translate in my spare time. One of the accountants had asked me over for a dinner party at his flat and I decided to go. I could do with a bit of company.

On the Monday, Boutonnet's secretary summoned me just before lunch. Monsieur Boutonnet was pacing up and down his office. He pointed to a chair when I entered, and I sat. He stood by the window, hands clasped behind him, not looking in my direction. At length, he positioned himself behind his desk, palms on its surface, fingers drumming. He examined my face with a severe expression. I started to speak, to break the silence, but he held up his hand.

'Where is the draft report I requested?'

'I thought you said, "if possible", and I haven't had time.'

'You have not had time?'

'No, monsieur.'

'I see.'

I felt indignant at this treatment but was surprised to hear myself saying, 'I have a life outside work.'

'Monsieur! Your tone borders on the insolent, not to say insubordinate.' There was another long difficult silence.

Finally he said, 'When the company's business demands it, there is no life outside the company. Are we clear?' He shook his shirt cuffs out of his jacket sleeves. 'I require the draft by close of business. Failing which I will consider you to be in breach of a direct order.'

I nodded, and as I withdrew I noticed the scuffmarks on the off-white wall at the level of the bicycle's handlebars.

I wrote my report in English, pulling no punches about the impracticability of machine translation. I added a bland executive summary in French to save Boutonnet the trouble of struggling through the whole thing: he'd only be anxious at the trenchant tone. Late that afternoon, I took it to his office. He was shuffling papers into neat piles. Without looking up he indicated that I should leave the document on his desk.

He never came back to me with comments or suggestions for revision; I suspect he barely glanced at the report, that his demand for a draft was nothing more than an assertion of status. A couple of days later, he reminded me to let him have the final version by the 25th. I asked what changes he would like. He said, 'Monsieur, we pay you as a professional to use your own initiative. So use it.'

The day of the meeting with Chrétien arrived. Boutonnet was a pitiful sight, patrolling his small territory, chewing on his lip, shrugging his neck, coming out of his office countless times to make trivial requests of his secretary. He poked his head round the door of my cubby-hole and said, 'Is everything ready?'

'Yes.'

'I hope so. All contingencies must be accounted for, *vous comprenez?*'

I nodded. He stood for a moment, blinked at me, and left.

Chrétien's office was on the nineteenth floor. It had large windows on two sides, and a panoramic view of the city's skyline. We were summoned to take our places in front of his desk while he sat behind it on an intimidatingly ergonomic black-leather chair. Up close, he was as jovial as a good-humoured crocodile, relaxed and at ease, but waiting to strike. He had a large oblong face and a cynic's eyes behind black-rimmed spectacles. He rested one shoe casually on the edge of the desk. My report lay in front of him. While we waited to begin he flicked through the pages, occasionally compressing his lips as if in disagreement or raising his eyebrows in surprise. He'd mark a passage with a highlighter, or stick a post-it note in place on a page, or look up to scrutinise us with his sharp grey eyes. Within easy reach on the desk was a red and gold packet of Dunhill cigarettes.

Boutonnet was as nervous as a spooked horse. He crossed and uncrossed his legs, ducked and twisted his head, and seemed to scrunch in on himself, arms folded, as if trying to hold himself together. An underling came in to take notes, and a representative of the computer planning department sat alongside us. Chrétien's secretary brought coffees. Boutonnet's hand trembled as he lifted his cup. His eyes darted around, from me to the secretary to the note-taking underling, but did not meet the gaze of *Monsieur le directeur.*

Chrétien got the meeting under way with a brisk, 'Good. Let's begin.' He asked for a summary. Boutonnet stuttered over his words, spouted non sequiturs, went on too long. He was gurning in confusion, his long, bony fingers winding round each other. Chrétien was getting visibly irritated, picking up the Dunhill packet, twirling it in one hand, flicking it back onto the desk. Boutonnet was muttering something incoherent about budgets, timescales and possible technical obstacles.

'What are you saying,' interrupted Chrétien. 'That there are practical difficulties?'

'No, Monsieur Chrétien, I did not intend—'

'Well are there or aren't there?'

'Well...'

'And if there are, what are you going to do about them?'

Boutonnet was pulling obsessively with thumb and forefinger at the hairs of his moustache. He managed to point in my direction. 'Our translation professional will be able to go into technical detail.'

Chrétien fixed his saurian eyes on me. Sensing that he was ruled by logic and rationality, rather than by status anxiety, I said, 'As I detail in the report, machine translation will not work.'

'What?' said Chrétien with his domineering briskness. 'You're challenging my initiative?'

'Yes. Because it won't work. There are insurmountable practical obstacles and problems of principle. Investing in this will be pouring money down the drain. For example—'

'OK, OK,' said Boutonnet, 'I'm sure Monsieur Chrétien does not want to hear problems, he wishes to hear solutions.'

Chrétien held up his hand. 'Continue, monsieur,' he

said to me.

I explained the inability of machine translation to cope with the infinite ambiguity of real utterances. While I spoke, I was conscious of Chrétien's fingers probing at the packet of Dunhills. He took out a cigarette, waved it in the air then put it back in the pack. He pushed the onyx ashtray to the far edge of the desk out of his line of sight.

When I'd finished, he turned to Boutonnet, who shrank into his chair. 'Well, Claude?'

'I'm sure, *Monsieur le directeur,*' said Boutonnet, twisting his fingers so hard that they seemed in danger of snapping like twigs, 'we will find workarounds for these inevitable problems.'

*'Zut et merde alors!'* cried Chrétien. He balled his fist. I thought he was going to hammer it down on the desk. 'Have you not listened to one single word this young man has said to us?' He opened the report at a post-it note and jabbed the page with his forefinger. 'You've read this, I presume? *"Pricks and bottoms", "Bites et culs", "Bites et culs"! Oh là là!* For the love of God, Boutonnet, if it doesn't work, it doesn't work!' The coffee cups were rattling with the force of his words.

The meeting stumbled to its close. Chrétien ordered Boutonnet to relax his over-zealous monitoring of every translation.

'Sampling, Claude, that is the way forward for now.'

Boutonnet nodded miserably.

'And managerial measures against those translators who fail to reach the desired standard. Understood? Good.' With that, Chrétien dismissed us from his presence.

I felt sorry for Boutonnet, but my pity vanished as soon as we entered the lift. He turned on me. 'What possessed you, monsieur, to challenge the authority of Monsieur Chrétien, to expose me in front of him?' He muttered the word *'intolérable'* several times, his head jerking violently from side to side like a dog shaking a rag doll.

I went back to my office to complete a piece of translation

work that was due, and later that day went to deliver it to the secretary. She'd already left, so I tapped at Boutonnet's office door and entered. The fluorescent purple and black cycling gear was laid out on the desk, the pointy helmet on top of it. My boss was still in his navy blazer, sitting on the floor with his back to me. He was worrying at the chain of his expensive bicycle with his bony fingers. The chain had come away from the derailleur gears, and instead of being taut it was dangling slackly. Boutonnet did little shrugging jerks of his neck in its collar and shuffled his arms down inside his jacket sleeves to expose the shirt cuffs. He had streaks of black grease on the cuffs, as well as on the fabric of the blinds and on the carpet. He looked like a lost little boy who was bravely holding back his tears. Or a machine whose programme had become corrupted and whose random movements served no purpose.

I pretended that I'd not noticed him, and left his office before he could look round.

# Linger On

A Saturday afternoon in Paris, some British Council literary event in a grand building near the rue de Rivoli. Moulded high ceilings, the soft murmur of RP English. Oxbridge-educated gents in blazers and ties standing around chatting in the shafts of sunlight, home counties ladies in summer dresses offering guests glasses of wine in execrable French. I'd had very little sleep. I grabbed a second glass of wine from a lady with a tray. She said, 'Haven't you had one already?'

I nodded. 'Yes, cheers.'

As I raised the glass to my lips, the lady muttered an affronted, 'Well!', to no one in particular. I heard a female voice pronounce a Dutch expletive, comically offensive in its linking of an intimate body part and a nasty disease. I burst out laughing, and narrowly avoided spraying the English lady with a fine mist of claret.

I turned. The voice belonged to an attractive woman in her late twenties. She was grinning, observing me. I said, in Dutch, 'The Brits abroad. Very unedifying.'

She said, 'Jesus, she has a face like a dog's arse.'

'I shouldn't have wound her up by taking another glass of wine.'

She clinked glasses with me. 'Cheers, I'm Sonja. With a "j".'

'*Natuurlijk.*'

'You don't look like a Nederlander.'

'I'm not. I'm English.'

'You could almost pass for a *Hagenaar*, with your accent.'

'From The Hague? Is that a good thing?'

She smiled. With my lack of sleep and the heat of the afternoon sun through the high windows, the wine was going to my head.

'How come you speak Dutch?' she said.

41

'I lived there as a kid, my father worked in The Hague for a while. So it's one of my languages. These days I earn my crust as a translator, so...'

A knife tinkling on glass, an English voice calling, '*Mesdames et messieurs! Mesdames et messieurs!*' The talk was about to begin.

'Shall we go and have ourselves a beer somewhere?'

'Sure,' I said.

That was how it began.

Sonja was wearing no make-up, except for a little eyeliner; granny glasses that softened her sharp pale blue eyes; jeans, threadbare and faded. That first afternoon, we sat in a café and talked for hours. She worked in translation too, a conference interpreter. In my mind, therefore, brash, confident, a performer, in contrast to the shrinking violet that is the literary translator. There was something about the way she stood, the curve of her lower back, that seemed to say, *ik ben een heel seksueel wezen*: I am a very sexual being. Normally I would have been intimidated by such physical self-assurance, but I found I could relax with her, make her laugh. In the café, the other tables were filled with good-looking young couples. Alpha males were deploying their mating resources: deep voices, assertive body language, physiques signalling genes worth reproducing. I said to Sonja, 'Did you know that in the world of frogs, it's having a deep croak that gets you the females?'

'No, I didn't.'

'So what do you do if you don't have a deep croak?'

'Give up on sex?'

'No, that's the thing. You swim out to the centre of the pond where the water is coldest, and that makes your croak go deeper. So a wily beta frog can pretend to be an alpha male and get his share.'

Sonja leant forward, forearms folded on the table, 'And what kind of frog are you?'

'You'll have to find out,' I replied, in a forced, deep

voice, and she laughed.

We met again the following weekend; walked and talked, came upon the cemetery of Montmartre, wandered through, looking at the tombs of the famous. I paused at Stendhal's grave. Even the bronze plaque on his gravestone did little to prettify him: the soul of a romantic in an unprepossessing body. The inscription read '*Scrisse, Amò, Visse*' – He wrote, he loved, he lived.

'So is that what you'll ask to be put on your tomb?' asked Sonja. She gave me a quizzical sidelong glance, as if to say that by the look of me I had quite a bit of writing, loving and living to get through before I qualified. I stammered something apologetic and ineffectual, but as we left through the imposing gates, Sonja put her arm through mine and invited me back to her place.

We took a taxi to a block of flats in a narrow street near Bir Hakeim and climbed the six floors to her duplex apartment. The rooms rumbled as the metro trains went over the bridge. She cooked steak and we ate, and drank wine, and it got late and I missed the last metro. We looked out of the window at the dark sky. She said it got cold at night.

'It being so high up,' she explained.

'Sure,' I said, 'Like a mountain top.'

'Yuh,' she said. She put on a Lou Reed CD and half-hummed, half-sang along: *Thought of you as my mountain top, Thought of you as my peak, Thought of you as everything I had but couldn't keep...*

She said I could stay; I said I'd sleep on the couch. She said I could share her bed because it got cold at night, it being so high up. I said sure, if she didn't mind.

In the early hours, in a state between sleep and waking, we found ourselves grabbing each other, exchanging fevered kisses. I remember her exact words, at the point at which we could no longer pretend we were asleep:

'*Het lijkt me dat we een beetje intiem zijn geworden.*' We seem to have got rather sexual. The fussy, precise little

43

expression sat oddly with the aroused huskiness in her voice.

'Yes,' I said. 'We do seem to.'

She stopped further conversation with a kiss that was both soft and fierce.

It took me all of two days to fall in love, for the first time in years. I was mesmerised by the way Sonja moved, by the way her eyes narrowed and glittered when she was about to say something controversial. By her warm attentiveness when we were together, her gaze fixed on me. By her fluent mastery of her demanding profession. By the way she found me amusing and clever. The way her voice, which could be harsh and forceful, or sarcastic and mocking, softened to a caress when she wanted to know how I was feeling.

With Sonja in my life, even the suffocating hierarchies of Electronica Inc, the American firm where I worked as a translator, seemed easier to bear. She was fun to be around, mischievous, with a capricious wind-chime of a laugh. When she realised that in my cramped one-roomed apartment you could hear every fart and sniffle from the next-door tenant – a man I'd never met – she started to exaggerate her orgasms, adorning them with synchronised growls, moans and shrieks in a quickening crescendo. Once, when the mystery man farted as if in response to her cries, we dissolved into such uncontrollable giggling that we couldn't resume love-making until we heard him go out, closing his front door loudly as if in reproach. Sometimes, she would fake an orgasm for her own amusement while drying the dishes or putting on her eyeliner.

Sonja worked at one of the big international organisations in Paris and was often called on for events in the evening or at weekends. And she'd fly off to conferences in Stockholm, New York or Istanbul for several days, sometimes longer. I was left on my own. I'd go on long walks to the smaller, quieter parks of Paris where I'd lie on the grass and pick at buttercups or chew stalks and want

44

to be with her.

Sonja's adventurousness, her outgoing optimism, made me feel cautious and gloomy in comparison. One of her passions was bouldering, *l'escalade*: short, tricky vertical climbs without ropes. She'd drag me with her to the forest of Fontainebleau where I'd watch her stretch her agile, spidery limbs into implausible shapes to grab a toehold or a fingerhold on a forbidding wall of rock. She'd place a small, light mat at the foot of the boulder, but it was clear to me that its value was symbolic, a nod to safety.

'Come on,' she would urge, 'give it a try. It's not that high.'

I felt trapped into compliance; I didn't want to appear a coward. She showed me where to place my fingers and toes, and called instructions up to me. 'Straighten your leg! *Straighten* it! Now reach out and up to the left. Left!' I tried to obey, but the wiring from brain to limbs seemed faulty, neurons failed to fire. 'Swap hands!' she yelled. 'Swap feet!' The manoeuvre was beyond me. I feared to look down. I was already too far from the ground to jump. 'Lean out!' she cried. 'Your arms will get tired holding yourself into the rock like that.' But, fearful of falling backwards, I could not lean out. And then, halfway to the top, the height of a room above the base of the boulder, I froze. I was unable to move in any direction. Sonja coaxed me down, hold by hold. Descending was harder than going up, the muscles in my thighs and shoulders screamed. My fingers were trembling. I half-jumped, half-slithered the last few feet, and fell awkwardly. I got up, bruised and exhausted but otherwise unhurt. Sonja seemed amused, but I felt humiliated by my own incompetence and funk.

A few months into our affair I went to collect her from work in a conference centre at the end of one of the RER train lines. She'd come off duty by the time I arrived, and insisted on showing me round the facilities. We left the lobby, where milling delegates were drinking coffee and eating pastries, and went into the empty conference hall. At the far end was a line of translators' booths. Sonja opened the door to one of them.

'Come on in, have a look,' she said. 'This is where I work.'

The booth had wide, tinted windows. On a desk that ran along the length of it was the paraphernalia of the conference translator. Sonja pushed back the set of fat headphones and the gooseneck microphone in its console, the spaghetti tangle of leads.

'The latest kit,' she said. 'See, it even has a replay button. In case you miss something. You can replay up to six seconds.'

'Then don't you miss something else?' I asked.

She leaned one buttock on the space she'd cleared on the desk, legs apart, her skirt hitching up her thigh. 'That's entirely possible, yes.'

'I mean, don't you miss six seconds of whatever the speaker...'

She took my hand and placed it high up on her thigh, her other hand round my neck, drawing me close. 'Yes, that's certainly something to worry about, isn't it. You'd never know what you were missing, would you?'

She began to unzip my flies. I was caught between desire and anxiety that we'd be interrupted. 'Someone could walk in,' I stuttered.

'They could but they won't. Not with refreshments out in the lobby. And if they did, they probably wouldn't even notice us.' She nuzzled into my ear, and whispered, all the time caressing me with her free hand, 'Didn't you know, interpreters are invisible? Mm?' She was easing my hand up under her skirt. 'Most delegates don't realise we exist, they think it's some kind of black magic.'

'Sonja...'

'And anyway. Isn't that part of the thrill?'

'Not really.'

But she took my lower lip between her two lips, and brushed the back of her hand down my stomach. 'I want it here, on this desk,' she said. She managed to loosen my trousers so that they fell to the floor, and she shuffled down her knickers and wrapped her legs around me.

I couldn't stop myself thinking that if we carried on, the next interpreter in post would surely notice an odour of sex coming from the surface of the desk. Sonja had just managed to draw me, at once willing and reluctant, into her when the headphones crackled, and a muffled voice said, 'One two three testing! One two three testing!'

She gripped me hard, but I'd lost it, I pulled away. She gave me a look, humorous but disappointed in me.

We were stalling in other ways too. She was going abroad on business trips more often. Having got used to her company, I resented her not being around.

I tried to make progress on my Peruvian novel translation. I was working on a passage in which a young man is arrested at random and taken to El Sexto prison. There, he's brutalised by sadistic inmates, unprotected by the guards. He's thrown into a cell with the common criminals and vagrants. When, sometime later, he's released, he's been so traumatised by his experience that within days he has returned to El Sexto, unable to function in the outside world where once he was a student of music. He spends his time playing an imaginary piano and singing melancholy Peruvian waltzes. In passages like these, the novel seemed so bleak that I wondered why I had set myself the task of translating it. Meanwhile, my day job at Electronica was unrewarding. My tiresome martinet of a boss would turn petulant when I tried to sidestep his more unreasonable demands. I felt trapped, wanting to hand in my notice but needing the income.

None of this really explains or excuses the fact that I slept with Trudy again, though it suggests my morose, pessimistic mood. Trudy was a young American, dark-eyed and sporty, also at Electronica, something to do with computers. I'd had a brief fling with her just before I'd met Sonja – a sort of colleagues-with-benefits arrangement. I started going out with Sonja, stopped seeing Trudy. It had seemed OK, but when I bumped into Trudy in the staff canteen she suggested hooking up again. 'You know, any time.'

'I'm sorry,' I said, 'I'm kind of taken.'

'Spoilsport,' she said.

Then in October Sonja went to Stockholm for ten days for a meeting of European economists. Missing her company, the sound of her voice, I tried to phone her mobile. It went straight to voicemail, and I imagined all sorts of things. I rang to leave a message for her at the hotel where she was staying, spelling out her surname. The receptionist said, 'Arendshof? I'm sorry, sir, we have no one called Arendshof currently on our system.'

There seemed to be no innocent explanation. When I'd heard nothing from Sonja two days later, I phoned the hotel again in case there'd been a mistake; there hadn't. The following day, I bumped into Trudy at work. 'Hey,' she said, 'if it isn't the elusive Englishman!' I should have smiled and moved on, but I stopped to chat.

'How's things?' I asked.

'Good. And you?'

'Good.'

'You're looking great,' she said.

'You too,' I said.

'So what are you doing this evening?'

'Nothing in particular.'

'Do you want to come and see *From Dusk till Dawn*? I have tickets.'

I shrugged.

'Is that a no?'

'Erm...'

'They'll only go to waste.'

'OK.'

So we went to see *From Dusk till Dawn*, which was called *Une nuit en enfer* in French, *A Night in Hell*. It was a blood-soaked vampire-action-horror flick, sub-Tarantino in style. In the gory bits, Trudy grabbed my hand and buried her face in my chest. Then she put her hand on my thigh and left it there, and I did the same. I felt strangely disassociated, as if I was watching myself do these things. I went back to her flat and we spent the night together. As I left after breakfast, she pulled me back and kissed me again, and said, 'Don't be a stranger.'

I felt bad afterwards, but also self-justifying. Sonja, unreachable in Stockholm, had clearly been up to no good. Going out with Trudy seemed, on some warped logic, fair in the circumstances.

Sonja returned the following week. I went round to her flat. She was warm and affectionate, stroked my face, kissed me, suggested we go to bed after a celebratory glass or two of red wine. All seemed fine.

I was shocked by the speed with which things unravelled.

As we drank I kept making digs about how she'd been off the radar in Sweden. She ignored me. Feigning innocence, I supposed. I hinted that I'd guessed the reason for her radio silence. I expected her to stand her ground and brazen it out in her usual fierce-frank way. Tell me to grow up, for God's sake. Tell me that, OK, she'd shagged the German-Swedish interpreter or the organisation's director of sustainable technology or some other opportunistic passing male, but so bloody what, no big deal, we weren't tied to each other body and soul. And then laugh, order me not to be a jealous baby, and kiss me.

She didn't do any of those things. Instead she said in a small voice, 'I'm very surprised you have so little trust in me.'

'I didn't say that. I just asked why I couldn't get hold of you.'

'I was working. Why would you want to get hold of me?'

'What about the hotel?'

'What *about* the hotel?'

'You weren't there.'

'No, we changed hotels.'

'*We?*'

'Yes, me and the other interpreters.'

'Sure!' I said. I didn't mean it to come out quite as sarcastic.

'Why are you interrogating me?' She pushed her glass away. 'Is it your guilty conscience, maybe?'

I was cut by her tone. I'd drunk three large glasses of wine by this point, too quickly. It was almost as if I wanted her to know that I was out there, able to play the field. 'Fair enough,' I said, 'it's true I haven't been entirely virginal while you were away.'

She looked at me, saw that I was not joking. Her eyes welled. She shook her head, covered her face with her hands, and sobbed. She'd caught me off guard. I got up and went to put my arm around her shoulder. 'I'm sorry, Sonja, I'm really sorry, it didn't mean anything, I just...'

But she shrugged my arm away and shouted, 'Don't touch me! Don't you dare touch me.'

I felt sick. 'Sonja, I've totally misread—'

'Why are you even still here! I don't want to see you. I'd like you to go now.'

'I'm so sorry, I didn't realise... I'll call you, maybe tomorrow or—'

'I don't want to see you now, or at all. Just go.'

We did meet up, once, to talk things over, at my request. Only a work colleague, I said, some American woman I knew from the office, there had been nothing to it. But the thing Sonja and I had was broken, irreparably; she was more upset by the fact I'd doubted her than that I'd fucked the American.

After that I didn't see her again for a decade. Then I ran into her at an international conference on literary translation in Seville. I hardly recognised her. She came up to me, took a confirmatory glance at my name badge with a neat little bend of the knees and dink of her head.

No amusing opening expletive this time, no *scheetje* or *drolletje*. Just a 'Hey! I thought it was you. How are you doing? Been a long time.' She embraced me briefly, an air kiss to each cheek and one for luck. She'd aged well. She was still very attractive, and had become chic: hair voguishly short, lipstick, careful make-up, contact lenses. The way she stood, though, with that enticing curve of the back, that was still the same, arousing in me a pang of longing, an intense desire to become once more *een beetje intiem* with her. But the cool, self-possessed gleam in her pale blue eyes told me that there was no chance of that.

# THE GILDED CAGE

The Trudy business blew up when I'd been in Paris for a few months, and it all became more complicated than I'd imagined. It began when one of my colleagues at Electronica, Guy Verga, invited me to a soirée at his flat. He'd asked me a couple of times before, and I'd declined. But it seemed impolite to refuse yet again.

Guy was a soft and plump young Belgian, the sort my ex-partner Rachel would have dismissed as 'caponised'. There was something clammy about him. He always had a faint sheen of sweat at the roots of his slicked-back hair. He chewed his fingertips, had a habit of rubbing his palms together, and pontificated. The company, he said, was '*une cage dorée*'. A gilded cage. Once you got in, it was hard to get out. What detained you wasn't bars and guards, but money, perks and status. In return, the company expected you to devote yourself to its service.

I got to Guy's place around eight o'clock. It was in a chic modern block in the south-west of the city. Guy opened the door and gave me one of his damp handshakes. He was dressed down, in a striped shirt, clashing tie and chinos. 'Hello, pleased you could make it!' he said in his American-accented English. 'Let me fix you a drink.'

I went through to the living room. It was decorated with a charmless minimalism: a couple of ostentatious black leather settees, deep-pile white rugs on the parquet, monochrome abstracts on the walls. Ten or twelve men and women were milling about with champagne flutes in their hands, well-groomed young professionals. I knew several of them from the office. Guy had prepared little canapés. He handed them round as if they were cordon bleu confections. I sensed a brittleness to the proceedings; we were stuck on the uncomfortable borderline between work and play. The flow of champagne did not loosen the atmosphere but gave it a febrile edge. By nine o'clock,

Guy was tottering as he made his rounds. His forehead glistened. People gave the impression they were waiting for something disagreeable to happen. I wondered why we had all come. Perhaps the others were asking themselves the same question. At the back of my mind was the draft report on machine translation that my boss Boutonnet was expecting by Monday, and I rather wished I'd stayed at home to work on it.

Cheeses appeared. Guy presented them, as if introducing honoured guests, alternately rubbing his hands together and clasping them to his chest. 'A little Beaufort, *chalet d'alpage*, very floral, very suave... And this Le Salers, explosive, animal. At least, that's what the *fromager* told me, ha-ha.'

'More bangs for your bucks,' said Trudy, an American woman I knew by sight. She worked on the same floor as me at Electronica.

'I hope so, it was a lot of bucks, for sure!' said Guy.

Trudy approached me. 'Hi, and where are you?' she asked.

'I'm right here.'

'You know what I mean.' She poked me in the ribs. 'I'm from computing projects and planning. What about you? Not another accountant like Guy, I trust?'

'No. Translator.'

'So you work with Boutonnet?'

'Yes.'

'Uh-oh. Good luck with that one.'

'Meaning?'

'The worst gig in the office.' She took a bite of cracker and Salers, and I caught a whiff of its explosive animality.

'He's—'

'You're telling me!' she said. 'Your typical drill sergeant. Has he bawled you out yet?'

'No.' I smiled. 'Not seriously, not yet.' On Monday no doubt he would, with my draft report unwritten.

'And of course, he takes—'

54

Trudy didn't get to finish her sentence. Guy had clapped his hands for attention and shouted, 'OK, girls and boys, it's show time!' He ushered us through a sliding partition to the far end of the lounge where he'd set up a screen and projector. People sat cross-legged on the white carpet, nursing their wine glasses. Guy turned out the lights.

'Right, we all take our clothes off, yes!' shouted Guy.

There were murmurings.

Trudy, who was sitting next to me, got to her feet. 'Jesus Christ, not this again.'

On the screen, a naked woman appeared, astride a man, sliding herself up and down with hypnotic regularity. Trudy and most of the other women had retreated through the sliding doors. I stayed for a while and watched as a succession of men and woman, fat and thin, white and black, amazingly hairy and almost hairless, engaged in varieties of copulation, with no build-up, just straight to it. They all seemed curiously unmoved, not a man or woman among them letting down their guard enough to be caught out in ecstasy or even to appear averagely happy, or amused, or even distressed. When a couple sat on a sofa and indulged in thirty seconds of foreplay prior to penetration, it seemed quaint and sweet. I got up and went back through the sliding doors, leaving Guy still trying to persuade the one remaining woman to take off her clothes.

'Exciting?' Trudy said.

'Oh, totally,' I said. 'Is he always like this?'

'Always.'

'So why do you keep coming?

She shrugged. 'I don't know. Esprit de corps? We all eat, live, sleep Electronica Inc, don't we?'

'Not really,' I said.

A few days later, I saw Trudy in the staff refectory. She called out, 'How's it going, *monsieur le traducteur?*'

'Good. Thanks.'

'Enjoy the movie show the other night?'

I glanced at her lunch companions, but they didn't seem

to sense a subtext. 'Quite stimulating, thanks,' I said. 'A bit shallow maybe, lack of plot or character development, but I guess it did what it said on the tin. Quite penetrating in that sense.'

'Oh, you men!' said Trudy.

She crossed her legs. I sensed mutual interest. One of her colleagues looked up from her meal and scrutinised me.

After her colleagues had left the canteen, Trudy said, 'You know, the thing about those porn flicks is that they're pretty disappointing. Everything done by the book, there's a formula, so impersonal.'

'Yes,' I said, 'it's all very problematic, isn't it. Raises all sorts of gender and exploitation issues.'

'Oh yeah?'

'Yeah. So why don't we have a civilised conversation about it over a glass of wine sometime.'

'O-kay...' she said, with that peculiar, long-drawn-out rising inflection that Americans use to express doubt or scepticism.

'So maybe not such a great—'

She cut in quickly, 'You're still just about educable I guess. How about this evening?'

'Yes, fine, why not?' I said.

'I'll change out of these' – she pointed to her high heels – 'and we can go for a walk. I'm down near Arts et Métiers.'

'I rather like the high heels.'

'In that case, buddy, you're very welcome to wear them,' she replied as she rose from her chair and clacked out of the canteen.

Trudy worked late. It was nearly nine when we left. I was used to walking but she was gym-honed and fit, bustling along as if determined to expend every last calorie. We marched through the Marais and headed east, stopping at a bar for a couple of glasses of wine. She kept returning to the subject of the porno movies, enjoying my embarrassment. 'Do guys really get off on that stuff?'

'Well, erm, not really...'

'The women look bored, because they *are* bored, and their orgasms sound like cats being strangled.'

'For someone who wasn't watching, you seem to remember quite a bit about it.'

'Tackiness sticks in the mind.'

'Sure.' I smiled. She grinned back.

'So are you a habitual cat-strangler?'

'Occasional,' she said.

We set off again. The wine didn't slow her down at all. Soon we'd reached Place de la Bastille. I said, 'There are some good Latino clubs round here, if you like Latin American music.'

'Love it!'

'Shall we?'

'Yeah! I'm not in the office tomorrow.'

'Not going in on a Saturday? You're slacking.'

She took the remark at face value. 'No, actually. I take work home with me at weekends.' She saw my smirk and gave me a play punch.

The place was called Sol y Sombra. It was heaving, the clientele mostly Latin Americans dancing *cumbia*. Different bits of their bodies seemed to move to different interwoven beats. We danced, then sat in a corner with our drinks and some food. It was too loud for a proper conversation, but at one point Trudy leant in close and said, 'What are you thinking?'

'I'm thinking I'd like to spend the night with you.'

She smiled and said into my ear, 'Well, what's to stop you?' She stroked the back of my neck with her hand, and she kissed me. I worried that I'd eaten raw onions with my hamburger, but she didn't seem to mind. We left soon afterwards and went back to her tiny top-floor flat.

Trudy was disconcertingly direct when we made love. I was used to women who would muddle along, maybe with little gestures or groans, until more or less by chance we'd hit upon whatever it was that did it for them. But she insisted – maybe it's an American thing – on telling me exactly what she wanted where, for how long, and with what degree of frictional vigour. It was a bit like being in bed with a driving instructor. I was drunk enough for it not to put me off my stride. She was uninhibited in the sense that she went through the full repertoire of moves. I think I preferred my sex a bit more haphazard, there was something a bit too drilled about her, as if she'd read the manual and practised hard.

Next morning, neither of us wanted to make too much of what had happened but agreed that hooking up now and then would be good. The last thing in my mind was a steady relationship with someone who worked on the same floor as me at Electronica. I felt claustrophobic at the thought of it.

I got home around mid-morning (Trudy had work to finish off), downcast at the prospect of being on my own for the rest of the weekend. I told myself, without enthusiasm, that I would make progress with my translation. The Lima prison novel was bleak, powerful, and enough to make you want to slit your throat. I was trying and failing to come up with a consistent vocabulary to convey the nuances of the informal hierarchies of life in the jail: the political prisoners, the high-status gang leaders, the common criminals. I felt disheartened by the challenge of staying faithful to the text, but coming up with something that was universal enough to resonate with an English readership. There was probably a good reason why, three decades after its publication, *El Sexto* was still untranslated. Unable to settle to work, I checked my desk diary and discovered that I'd put my name down for a literary salon that afternoon. I snatched a couple of hours' sleep, showered, and set off.

This was the event where I met Sonja Arendshof, the conference translator from Amsterdam. For a few months, Sonja and I became an intense, inward-looking unit. While it lasted, nobody else could penetrate our bubble. Certainly not Trudy, though that didn't stop her trying.

'You're avoiding me!' she'd say, when I bumped into her at the office.

'I'm not avoiding you. Boutonnet has me chained to the desk, and whips me if I don't get my captivating reports to him on time. How's the computer planning department these days?'

'Great. Just fantastic. What are you doing tonight?'

'Er...'

'Fair enough. This is about your cheese-fed femme fatale, isn't it.'

'It's not about her, and don't—'

'Keeping you on a tight leash, is she? I thought Dutch women were more open-minded on such matters.'

'Hey, Trudy.'

'All right, don't get uptight, I'm kidding.'

'OK.'

And then she said, with unexpected bitterness, 'And don't try to make out I'm stalking you.'

'I'm not. Look, I've got to go, Boutonnet has summoned me.'

'So go.'

It was a few months later, in a momentary fit of pique at Sonja's unavailability, that I slept with Trudy again. Rather perversely, after Sonja had ditched me, Trudy and I began to see much more of each other, meeting up most weekends. There was never a romantic 'moment', a *coup de foudre*: we were casual, low-key, and had sex. I imagine she'd have said we were 'dating'. For me, the casualness was a soft landing after the emotional intensity of my time with Sonja. The fact that Trudy seemed shallow was an advantage. Maybe I also found it convenient to blame her, unconsciously, for the break-up and to use her as a focus for my anger.

Trudy implied she was OK with our loose arrangement, but I began to sense she wasn't. She'd want to cook at home and – as if we were a regular couple – invite round her

British and American cronies. These were usually people with whom I felt I had nothing in common. Or she'd expect me to sit down with her and watch awful French television programmes, or films. The movies she liked were mainly romantic comedies – *Pretty Woman, Four Weddings and a Funeral, Green Card* – the sort of thing I loathed. The sex was good, but I found myself disliking the clingy look in her unmade-up eyes first thing in the morning, as if she didn't want me to leave. I sensed she wanted me to say affectionate things to her during love-making, and not pull away soon afterwards, but lie with her in the wet patch, my arm around her. Once I said, 'Maybe we're... it's getting, you know, a little intense.'

'Speak for yourself, I'm cool,' she replied. 'I know we're fuck buddies, nothing more.' That was the first time I'd heard the expression. Fuck buddies. I was OK with that.

But at work, I found it hard to get her to maintain a professional distance. She would sidle into the staff canteen a minute or two after I got there, or be lurking in the coffee lounge at my usual break time. I saw her in the corridors near our department, and she began coming in to chat to the secretary, which she'd never done before. Once, I was sitting on a sofa in a deserted reception area and she appeared, as if by chance, sat down next to me and started talking about work things: 'I mean – Jesus! – did you go to that presentation? HR are the pits. I'm not sure I'll still want to work here if they go ahead with the new policy.' The whole time she was gazing at me, her face close to mine, and rubbing her fingers up and down my stomach. I was aroused and repulsed at the same time.

'Kiss me.'

'No! Not here, Trudy. It's a public place, it's unprofessional.'

'Fuck them. They can see us, I'm not ashamed.'

'It's not that... After work, fine.'

'You're such an asshole.'

The next time I saw her, she brushed the whole thing

off, said I was exaggerating, denied she'd been touching me up in public, claimed she'd only wanted a peck on the cheek. But soon she began again with the quietly insistent demands for attention. She was taking up more of my spare time, and I found it hard to work on my literary translation. In hindsight, Trudy gave me just the pretext I needed to escape from it: I could blame her for my failure to make progress.

After a weekend trip to London, I came back to my little studio flat near the Avenue de Clichy, sat at the desk, and stared at the closed box file of typed notes on the Peruvian novel. With its marbled charcoal-grey pattern, the file seemed forbidding, impregnable. I shoved it aside in frustration. I stood up and looked down at the neat gardens and the railings, listening to the birds – normally you can't hear birdsong in Paris – and realised that Trudy and I had reached the end of the road.

I arranged to meet her that Saturday night, in a bar near Arts et Métiers. 'I want to call a halt. I mean, to what we had. It's been good, very good, but I no longer feel comfortable with...' As I spoke I realised I was talking like I imagined some character in an American soap would talk, trying to speak a language I supposed she'd understand. Time to move on, to free both of us up to grow and change, and—

'Just cut the bullshit!' she said. She berated me for my selfishness and insensitivity, sniffled a bit. 'I feel abused. You're a bastard.'

'Look, we have to carry on working together, we both knew the score when—'

'"*Knew the score*?" Knew the fucking score? What does that even mean! And by the way, no we don't, we don't have to continue working together. In fact, you hanging around the office would be like harassment.'

'That's ridiculous.'

'I don't have to move on. *You* have to move on. Find yourself another place to fool around, buddy.' That word, 'buddy', again, and not in an erotico-friendly context.

'I'm not moving on, it's my job.'

'I can make life hell for you,' she said.

'I don't doubt it.'

'I'm fucking serious.'

'I know. Look, can we go and talk about this somewhere more private.'

'You and your fucking privacy! I don't give a damn if they hear us. I want you to go, leave Electronica. Hand in your notice.'

I thought she was going to say, 'I was there first!'

She started crying again. I said, 'This is pointless.'

I went into the office on Monday morning and stayed hidden in my cubicle most of the day. I kept looking anxiously to where the secretary sat, expecting Trudy to appear. But there was no sign of her. On Tuesday, Guy Verga came up to me in the coffee lounge with an eager solemnity. 'You heard about Trudy?'

I felt prickles in my scalp. 'No. What about her?'

'Oh, I thought you and she were... She's in hospital.'

'Christ.'

'She took an overdose.'

'Jesus!'

'So you didn't hear?'

'No, this is the first I've... And is she... will she be OK?'

'I guess so, they pumped her stomach, somebody said.'

'Jesus Christ.'

I'd been blind to the warning signs. I agonised for days about going to see her in the hospital up near the Gare de l'Est, telling myself it probably wasn't the best thing for her given her state of mind. I also loathed everything that (in my imagination) went with a failed suicide attempt: the medical paraphernalia of lines and pumps; the wheeze and whine of the machines; the smell of vomit and disinfectant. I visualised the ghastly unmade-up pallor of her face.

In the end I did go to visit her, once, at the hospital.

She was too exhausted to discharge the full force of her emotional distress on me, and lay unresponsive, staring into space. She murmured something repeatedly in a hoarse voice until a nurse came in and gave her a sip of water. I left quickly.

Once she'd been discharged, I didn't go to see her, nor did I bump into her around Electronica. Sometime later, Guy told me she'd left to take up a job at another US company, near La Défense. 'She'll be earning half what she was taking home here, and they don't have anything like the benefits. Weird.'

About three months after we'd broken up, with the leaves on the trees in the Cité des Fleurs changing colour and the light evenings shortening, I received a handwritten letter at my home address. It was in her slightly childish handwriting, looping and precise. She said not to get in touch. The letter was angry and raw. *This was not about you, this was about me. Not everything is about you and your insecurities/needs and you being so wrapped up in yourself. I don't think you actually realise how emotionally stunted you are and how much you've hurt and used me... Do you behave like this with all the women in your life?'* It rambled on in this vein over two sides, ending, 'Yrs, Trudy'. There was no return address.

Maybe what she said changed, a little, my view of her. Despite her svelte American angularity, her choreographed bedroom proficiency, her literalness, she was a more complicated, passionate woman than I'd given her credit for. I wished I could have felt more emotionally engaged, more connected to her, than I did. I put the letter down on the desktop. Behind it, unopened for weeks, lay the box file of the translation notes. There was even a film of dust on the top of it, which I wiped at with a finger before pushing it right to the back of the desk.

Philippe was one of the few people from work I could hold a decent conversation with. In the weeks before I met Sonja, we'd been out together a couple of times for a few beers. I'd mentioned that my cousin, who was almost like a brother, was coming to Paris for the long weekend. 'Bring him round,' Philippe had said. 'We'll have a light supper, and I'll see if I can get a couple of other friends over.'

So, that Friday evening, my cousin Mark and I walked from my place in Épinettes to Philippe's little studio flat off the rue de Clichy.

'You've got bags under your eyes, Mark,' I said.

'I know. Been up since five this morning to get the plane. Not to mention working bloody hard, commissions to finish, deadlines.'

'And playing hard?'

'Possibly. You know what London's like.' He grinned. He was not currently in a serious relationship – 'time out', as he put it – and was enjoying the freedom, in his thirties, to behave like a twenty-something again. 'Don't worry,' he assured me, 'I'll perk up if there's some action.'

We got to Philippe's flat, the sort of quirky, charming place that in the mid-nineties you could still just about find in Paris with a bit of luck and the right contacts. Philippe inspected us as if searching for differences. 'I can see there's a family resemblance,' he said.

'We're first cousins, born ten days apart, our mothers are sisters,' I said.

'So we could almost be twins, no?' said Mark. He stood tall to emphasise the several inches' disparity in height between the two of us, and brushed back his floppy light-brown hair, which made him look younger than he was – certainly younger than me.

We were born in the same month in the same year, though in different countries. I didn't meet Mark until I was nearly six, when my family moved back to London from the Netherlands. Our first meeting was dramatic. Our mothers sent us to the garden to play while they caught up. Mark even then was much lankier than me, and more outgoing. He said, 'Come on, we'll charge, like bulls.' He stood me at one end of the garden and went to the other. *'Chaaarge!'* he cried, and came galloping towards me at full tilt, head down, hands to his temples like horns. I did the same. We met in the middle, crunchingly, skull to skull, and collapsed to the grass. 'That was brilliant!' he said, while I lay on the lawn, my head pounding. My own half-siblings were much older than me, and I saw little of them, while Mark was an only child. Which was no doubt why he and I became and stayed firm friends through school. We kept in touch when we went off to different universities, met up in the holidays, saw each other when we were both working in London.

So we sat at Philippe's little square dining table. We felt slightly uncomfortable. Philippe opened a bottle of wine. On the table were a couple of books and a glazed bowl, about the only decoration in the room. The books were novels in English.

'Any good?' I asked, lifting the top one up. I knew Philippe enjoyed reading English fiction to hone his language skills: important if he wanted to advance his career in the training department at Electronica.

'I'm about to give up on this. It's a stream of consciousness in a sort of slangy Glasgow dialect, and I don't know what in hell's name is going on. It won some big prize in the UK.'

'The Booker?'

'That's it. Perhaps you could do a translation. An English language version.'

'I don't speak Glaswegian.'

He pointed to the other book. 'But this one here is magnificent. Also won the Booker a couple of years ago. *Sacred Hunger.* Which is the lust for profit. It's about capitalism, colonialism, enslavement...'

'So, a history of Electronica?'

'No, it's...' He saw my grin. 'Ah, yes, could well be!' Mark, who was not much interested in literature, was absently fingering the rim of the bowl. It seemed enormous on the square tabletop, its sides sloping steeply in so that it looked unbalanced with its wide top and narrow base. It was white, with an indigo whirl spiralling round the interior to the bottom. In it were a couple of shrivelled tangerines and a speckled banana. I reached out to feel the cool glaze. Philippe said, 'Hey, watch this.' He tipped out the fruit and started to rotate the bowl slowly, the indigo whirl creating the illusion that it was drawing you down into the depths.

Mark peered over my shoulder. He said, 'Neat.' I moved my head in a slow circle to clear it of the slightly dizzying effect of the pattern.

Philippe went across to the stove to prepare the food, leaving us the bottle of red. I noticed that Mark was stifling yawns, and I prodded him surreptitiously with my foot. But he became more animated after a glass of wine. In a few minutes we smelt the perfume of peppercorns, and meat on the griddle.

'How do you like your steak?' Philippe shouted.

'Still breathing,' said Mark. 'But only just.'

My cousin spoke quite good French, for an engineer, having spent six months in Paris in the 1980s on a student exchange. His offbeat, exuberant style won people over. Or alienated them, it was hard to tell in advance which it would be. I was always more reserved. More buttoned-up, Mark would say. He tended to just go for it. Which was probably why we were so close, for cousins: our differences bound us together.

As Philippe was bringing the plates to the table, the entry buzzer sounded. 'That will be *les nanas*,' he said. *The girls.* Over his shoulder he added that they were from a branch of his family in Alsace, and in Paris to study. The

67

buzzer went again, a longer pulse. 'Coming!' he called, pointlessly, and he pressed the button to open the entry door to the building.

*Les nanas* were gorgeous sisters in their mid-twenties, wearing miniskirts, and with the sort of thick, rippling, casually groomed hair that only the stunningly attractive and privileged can sport. They had an icy self-assurance, the hauteur of women who had long since learned to disregard the male gaze. The younger one, Sandrine, had a shimmering, barely contained sensuality. Mark couldn't take his eyes off her. Delphine, the older, was skinnier, more intellectual-looking, with an angular face and restless eyes. They sat down, Sandrine on the sofa, Delphine at the table. The two sisters crossed their legs, as if in unison, flicked their lovely manes, and looked about them in a way that managed to suggest both boredom and an aloof awareness of their surroundings, including Mark and me.

Philippe made the introductions and poured the sisters a glass of white wine each. Delphine took the Glasgow novel and made a roll-up on it. When she spoke, she addressed the tobacco, barely bothering to raise her eyes. I gathered they were living in a posh apartment in the *seizième*. They paid no rent as the property belonged to an uncle who spent nine months of the year on the Cote d'Azur. The sisters declined food and watched us eat, expressionless.

Mark finished his steak quickly, put down his cutlery, and angled his chair towards Sandrine. He began chatting easily in his colloquial French, brushing a flopping hank of hair from his forehead, as if unconsciously mirroring the sisters' flicks. Sandrine's face softened into veiled amusement, and Mark moved from the table to sit beside her on the sofa, turning his upper body towards her. He told her he was a designer of bridges, evaluating loads, materials, tensile and compressive forces. Joining the fingertips of both hands, he explained what happened if you got your calculations wrong, cited dramatic bridge disasters. His speech was lubricated with shrugs and raised eyebrows, and extravagant rocking gestures to convey the impact of high winds.

The buzzer sounded again. Philippe went to the entry phone, and his voice had a note of inquiry. In a moment he returned to the living room with a striking dark-haired man in his mid- or late twenties, even taller than Mark, with burning black eyes and a powerful presence, like an odour.

'This is Mathieu, an old friend from when I was working in Canada,' said Philippe. 'His first visit to Paris, I believe.' He turned to the newcomer. 'Did you find your way easily?'

'Yes, of course,' said Mathieu. I could see the two sisters watching him. 'When I come to a new city, I study the street plan, systematically, until I can orient myself from memory. Paris is more complicated than Montréal. But it's child's play compared with Marrakesh or Tokyo.' He spoke French with a pungent French-Canadian accent, and his eyes flitted to Sandrine and back to Philippe. He was quite conscious of the effect he was having.

'A drink?' said Philippe.

'Something non-alcoholic,' said Mathieu. He sat down opposite me at the table and gave a curt nod. He picked up *Sacred Hunger* just long enough to register that it was an English novel before tossing it back on the table with disdain. Turning his head diagonally towards Sandrine on the sofa, he fixed her for a moment with a stare, blatant and predatory, and she flicked her honey-coloured hair again, her eyes briefly engaging with his. In her look there was a kind of sullen interest. It was as if they were acting out a choreographed routine.

Mark prickled with irritation. He'd seen her first, and he'd need to perform a spot of scent-marking. I felt a rush of social anxiety, because Mark was not adept at polite restraint. Sure enough, he started to pepper his conversation with crude imitations of Mathieu's French-Canadian accent and idioms.

69

Philippe asked Mathieu if he was hungry. He replied, in his brusque manner, 'No, I've eaten recently.'

'*Poutine*, I imagine,' said my cousin, referring to the down-market fare of French fries with sauce found in greasy-spoon cafés throughout French-speaking Quebec. Mathieu gave him a contemptuous, cold-eyed look. Mark converted the moment into a comical playground staring match. Meanwhile, Sandrine was murmuring, '*Ah, mais moi,* j'adore *la poutine!*', though I doubt anything as unwholesome as a French fry had ever passed those perfect lips.

Philippe, playing the mediator, insisted that the English humour had been lost in translation, that no malice was intended.

'*Si,*' Mark muttered under his breath: Yes, it *was* intended.

Philippe tried to guide the conversation onto safer ground, asking Mathieu what he was up to these days. It turned out that he was working as a journalist for a newish Canadian magazine, writing opinionated pieces on culture and social mores in places around the Francophone world, earning very little and suffering for his art. But he had plans to set up his own French-Canadian literary journal, *Le Dépanneur*, publishing experimental fiction, philosophy, politics: a challenge to the linguistic and cultural hegemony of English.

As Mathieu spoke, I could see Mark becoming even more irked, especially as Sandrine was now paying serious attention to the *Québecois*. 'That sense of vocation must be wonderful!' she breathed. 'I'd adore to be a journalist, or at least a writer of some kind.' She leaned forward on the sofa, winding her legs round each other, her lashes long, like a veil for her fine chestnut-coloured eyes.

Desperate to break into the conversation, Mark said, 'And what about science in your new publication? You're not going to completely ignore the sciences or engineering, surely?'

Mathieu looked at him, as if at an annoying insect. 'Science is prosaic, dull. I know science. As for engineering... It's for classrooms and industry. In Canada we don't need more industry. We have industry, we have Bombardier.' *Bombardzhié* it sounded like in his quaint French. 'But I am interested in the transcendent, the poetic, the abstract, the fluid. Not in reinforced concrete.'

'*Bravo!*' said Sandrine.

My cousin took the hit and retaliated. He said something like, '*Hostie de câlisse de tabarnak!*' with a passably good French-Canadian accent; how typical of him to be fluent in offensive Quebec profanities. The host, the chalice, the tabernacle: strong stuff. I shrank back in my chair.

Mathieu turned to Philippe with a menacing smile and said, 'And these are *friends* of yours?' Poor Philippe gave me a quick, despairing glance, an appeal to rein in my cousin.

Mark smirked, impudent and unrepentant. He yawned, and put the back of his hand to his mouth. I attempted to carry on as if nothing untoward was occurring, turning to Delphine, and asking her what she did in life. She was a postgraduate student of dance and drama, she said, occasionally deigning to glance in my direction, while her sister was studying for a Masters in anthropology. Her green eyes alarmed me. Physically, she was my type, though I could see I wasn't hers.

Mark filled his glass with wine. He was pleased with himself, yet also a little nervous that he'd gone too far, that Mathieu might be a dangerous adversary. Now he was chatting to Sandrine again. Mathieu had them both fixed in his molten glare.

I asked Delphine what kind of dance interested her. She gave me a brief and brittle smile and said to Philippe, 'Remind me where your bathroom is.' He pointed to a door at the far end of the attic space. Sandrine followed Delphine out, leaving Mark in mid-sentence, his eyebrows theatrically raised. He shrugged, yawned again and leaned back against the sofa. In a moment his eyes had closed. I've always envied him his ability to doze off anywhere, it was what kept him going in his frenetic life, I suppose.

*Les nanas* were gone a long time. Mark dozed on. Philippe, having put on a CD of some dreary Quebec *chanteuse*, sat down next to Mathieu. They were deep in conversation, their tones too low for me to catch. I thought I heard Mathieu refer to 'that clown of an engineer', but I was probably imagining it. I felt invisible. When the sisters returned, Mathieu caught Sandrine by the arm and whispered something to her. She smiled and looked at Mark, whose upper body had slumped to one side. His mouth was open, and his right arm dangled over the edge of the sofa.

I felt my anxiety building. It was often like this around Mark: he got himself into scrapes, went too far, placed himself at risk: physical peril, the prospect of humiliation. I was frequently saving him from himself, as I saw it, while he went blithely on. Like the time in primary school, kicking a football about in the playground. We'd have been seven or eight. Simon Bone, the over-sized bully from year six, turning up with one of his mates, trying to muscle us off 'his' pitch. Mark standing up to him, Bone grabbing him in a headlock.

I yelled, 'You leave my cousin alone!' To the surprise of both of us, Bone desisted.

I wanted us to scarper, but Mark picked up the ball, bounced it, and said, 'No. Next goal wins.'

As I sat in Philippe's apartment watching Mathieu and Sandrine whisper conspiratorially, seeing my cousin lolling on the sofa fast asleep, I realised I was clenching my jaw so tight my teeth hurt. Mathieu was saying, 'So, warm water, OK.' Sandrine nodded. Mathieu tipped the fruit out of the bowl, the bowl with the whirling spiral design, and handed it to her.

'What's going on?' inquired Philippe, glancing from Mathieu to Sandrine and back again. Mathieu ignored him.

'How warm?' Sandrine asked.

'Thirty-eight degrees Celsius.'

'How am I going to know...? Do I need a thermometer?'

'No, of course not,' Mathieu said. 'Tepid, blood temperature. When it doesn't feel hot or cold to your hand. Just neutral.'

'Oh,' Sandrine said, pouting. 'OK.' She went through to the kitchen, and I heard the tinkle of water changing tone as the vessel filled up. It made me think of the indigo pattern spiralling round, slipping into nowhere but never disappearing.

Sandrine returned, with small cautious steps, trying not to let the water swill and splash. 'Put it on the floor,' ordered Mathieu, 'next to the sofa.'

In my head, in my entrails, the indigo swirl rotated slowly.

'Please mind the carpet,' pleaded Philippe, 'the landlord is very...' He trailed off, at a loss, outgunned.

Delphine stayed seated and silent, watching proceedings with a lazy, unconcerned smile.

Philippe said, 'I don't see this as a good idea.'

'Yes, of course it is,' said Mathieu. 'He likes science, see it as a scientific experiment.'

I leaned in towards Delphine. 'What are they up to?'

She said, 'Well, you know...'

'What?'

'They say if you put someone's hand into a bowl of lukewarm water when they're sleeping...'

'Yes?'

Mathieu said, '*Now.*' Sandrine took Mark's flopping hand and was about to dip it into the water.

'The whole hand immersed to the wrist,' Mathieu said.

I suddenly grasped what it was all about. They wanted Mark to piss himself, there on the sofa. I imagined the damp stain seeping into the fabric of his beige chinos: Mathieu's revenge.

I called, 'Mark! Mark!' but he didn't stir. I got to him

just as Sandrine, realising that the dangling hand would not reach the water, was lifting the bowl to meet it. I pushed her hand away with my foot, and water sloshed out onto the floor. Caught by surprise, Sandrine set the bowl back down with a clumsy, alarmed movement and a little cry of '*Mais ça, alors!*' As the bowl touched the floor, it tipped onto its side. The contents gushed over the carpet, and within seconds I caught the ominous drip-drip as water filtered through the boards, no doubt into the ceiling lights of the flat below.

Mark awoke. He looked bemused by the chaos. Philippe was rushing around holding his hand to his head, searching in cupboards for mops and towels, and crying, 'For the love of God... What a disaster! The landlord's going to blow a fucking fuse!'

Mark said, 'Was I asleep? Where's my wine?' He waggled his eyebrows at Sandrine.

I said to Mark, 'Come on. We'd better go.'

'What, so soon? We've only just...'

But still groggy from sleep and alcohol, he was biddable, and I led him out of the flat, stammering my apologies, already wondering what I was going to say to Philippe at work on Monday. From the hallway I glimpsed Mathieu touching Sandrine on the shoulder as she crouched to mop the carpet, and she glanced up at him with a smile of connivance. On the lower landings, front doors were opening and neighbours calling: 'There's a leak! What's going on! Our lights have gone out!'

'Jesus!' I said when we were in the street, heading in the direction of my studio flat in the Cité des Fleurs. I explained to Mark what had happened while he'd been sleeping.

'Possibly I did kind of wind him up.'

'You did. Kind of.'

'But it was fun, no?'

'No,' I said, shaking my head.

'And Sandrine, she was hot. Even if she did try to make

me piss myself. Damn!'

'You're a bit old for her.'

'Bollocks! ... You reckon?'

It would be like this with Mark and me in ten years' time or twenty, I mused. I could see him remaining this carefree man-child well into middle age and beyond, with me as his plodding accomplice, or guardian. I smiled to myself with a secret, slightly queasy pleasure at the thought.

# The Hortus Botanicus

In the days when I was still with Rachel, I'd wake from the dream and get up and prowl the bedroom, have a drink of water. I'd get back into bed and wait to become drowsy again. I'd glance at Rachel asleep beside me. She'd lie in that pose of hers, the fingers of one hand cradling the tip of her nose, the other arm stretching out as if to make sure I was still there; and I'd feel reassured. But also depleted. Not quite who I was, or wanted to be.

Even these days the dream still comes, sometimes, and Rachel is long gone. Every time it happens I wake in a panic, and it takes me a while to realise I'm not still trapped in that courtyard in Paris, hemmed in by riot police, the truncheons flailing, my eyes raw from the tear gas. I got out. I got out. I take a deep breath, my heart rate slows. I become calmer. My jaw aches from clenching my teeth. Sometimes the dream repeats itself in a cycle, with variations on the theme: they come for me when I'm at work, or in bed, or in the park, they come for me with guns or dogs.

When I was a boy, I loved stories of escape, of getting out. There was something so exhilarating about the planning, the preparation, the setbacks, the final achievement: that relief, the ability to breathe again, to take in lungfuls of free air. I remember having, even in primary school, the intense feeling of being trapped in childhood, the sense that the desired state of adulthood was an intolerably long way off. Perhaps it was because my mother was too egotistical in her love, too anxious to protect me – the *nakomertje*, the afterthought, much younger than my half-siblings – against all conceivable dangers, and the unimagined ones.

Even small escapes seemed invigorating. In summer I'd run after school to the local park, with its fishing lake, woods and grass slopes, and play cricket there with my cousin Mark and our friends. Sometimes, my father would drive Mark and me out to the countryside. He was a jovial, compliant, easygoing man. But even he needed his escapes from a home where everything was regimented and rule-bound, the rules being set by my mother. Once, Dad took Mark and me to Hertford. We parked the Renault in sight of the castle and set out along a public footpath. It started to rain. The ground was squelchy with churned mud. At almost the furthest point of the walk, we came to a field of cattle.

'Don't worry,' said my father, 'they're only bullocks. Just look confident, like Mark.'

The animals turned to face us, as one. They sauntered forwards, then quickened their pace. Their heads went down. They came at full gallop.

'Run!' cried my father.

Mark and I were quicker than him and we skidded to the ground and slid under the lowest strand of a wire fence into the neighbouring field. Seconds later, my father joined us. We lay in the mud, breathing hard and gazing at each other in wonderment.

My father shook his head in mock disgust. 'You'd let your own dad be mown down by a herd of bulls! What do you think of that, Mark? Leaving his own dad to be trampled to death!'

'They're bullocks, not bulls,' I said. 'And you're still alive, aren't you.'

'That was brilliant!' said Mark.

We were all laughing. It seemed like a great adventure. We got back to the car, wet through, filthy, happy. Night was falling as we headed home. I sat in the front passenger seat and watched the broken white line of the road markings unspool before us into the darkness. I wanted us to drive on, not go home, and I yearned for the day when I could set off by myself, disappear into the night, feel free.

The idea of flight still thrills me, has secretly enlivened my staid relationships, has allowed me to bear the tedium of office jobs on which I depended for a steady income. I think that's why as a literary translator I was, perversely, drawn to that Peruvian prison novel, *El Sexto*. It held a horrid fascination for me. I had hoped my English version would be my calling card for entry to the world of literary translation. But with its claustrophobia, its litany of inhumanity and its hopelessness – no inmate escapes its confines – the novel was like the sum of all my fears. Which is why, I suppose, I never completed it. But neither was I ever able to throw away the bulging box file of notes and research, even when I'd long since given up working on it.

I've come to realise that things are more complicated. The thrill of escape is transient, there are trade-offs to be made. What if freedom is achieved through cowardice, like those men trampling over women and children to make it to the *Titanic's* liferafts? The trouble is you don't have time to think, fear kicks in, your old, reptilian brain takes over. That's a high price to pay. Or perhaps you escape only to find yourself trapped in some other, wider place of confinement.

That incident in Paris, in the courtyard of the Sorbonne, should have been the living out of my escape fantasy, but somehow it wasn't. It was two decades ago, an unsettled period in my life: after I'd come back from Paris, from that soul-destroying job at Electronica, to live in London again. I was scrabbling for work, and eventually found a job as a translator-cum-editor for a tiny politics review specialising in Southern Europe.

One weekend, I went to a party not expecting to know many people. And there was Rachel. I hadn't seen her for years. We'd gone out for about a year and a half, in a low-key sort of way, around 1990, 1991. It would have been following my return from Lima and before Paris. She moved to Manchester for a new job and our thing had petered out. We both started seeing other people, and lost touch. I remember feeling relieved; she'd always seemed to want more out of it than I did.

79

But then, that party. I was morose and rather lonely at the time, discombobulated by my stint at Electronica and my gross ineptitude at relationships. I watched Rachel in motion, animated, funny, sociable, dancing to Daft Punk and Ricky Martin. She was one of those people who could dance and be sensual without trying too hard. And, forgetting how I'd come to find the relationship cloying and oppressive, I thought, 'Why did we ever break up?' She saw me, waved, and came over. We embraced, got talking. Stayed late, exchanged numbers. Started going out again.

For a while we rubbed along pretty well. She taught English to immigrant children, many of whom had escaped traumatic lives, and she was evangelical about it. But in many ways we had little in common. She adored dogs (I disliked them) and doted on her ill-disciplined liver-coloured Labrador, Ollie; was a keen gardener and loved houseplants (I was indifferent to them); doodled naff flowers around her name on scraps of paper; enjoyed inane television panel shows; was a born home-maker, and loved children (I disliked them). In company, she dominated proceedings with her high, bright schoolteacher's voice, rattling on amusingly about clothes and work and holiday plans and TV programmes. And I'd grow reserved and silent, turn into an observer.

Rachel's favourite pastime of an evening was to curl up next to me on the sofa and watch TV. She'd reach out a hand and place it on my arm and squeeze, as if to reassure herself I was still there. She'd let Ollie jump up and lick her face until I could stand it no longer and would shut him in the kitchen. He'd scrabble at the door, making pitiful whining noises. At which point I was expected to take him for long night walks. 'I think you've traumatised him,' Rachel said, 'poor Ollie.'

A few months after we'd started going out again, she began spending much more of the week at my one-bedroomed flat in Stoke Newington. Her father was ill at the time. They operated on him and it went well, but she needed my support: mainly listening to her while she talked about how she felt and what it would be like if he died. I tried to be sympathetic even after it was clear he was on the mend and would survive. And then, after about nine months, she basically moved in with me. One day, she offered to pay half the rent. I said, 'But you'll be paying two rents.'

She said, 'No I won't, not if I give up my lease.' When I hesitated she became tearful and started talking about her father, and I felt like a cad. Then we made love.

I felt tricked, but she knew how to play on her sexual attraction. Unlike Trudy she did not sound like an instruction manual in bed, and knew how to make me laugh. When she came, she growled low, like an angry wild creature, a lynx maybe, which I have to say turned me on.

Then, having moved in with me, she started saying we should think about finding somewhere bigger, with a garden, and a spare room. It was hedged about with ifs and maybes, but I began to feel trapped by her demands. She wanted to be with me all the time, go off on romantic trips. It was suffocating.

'Let's get away together before Christmas,' she said.

'I've already told Mark I'd go somewhere with him for a couple of days.'

'Your *cousin* Mark?' She had met Mark, and didn't much care for him. She thought him a chancer. 'Can I come?'

'What, the three of us? That would be a bit—'

'Where are you going?'

'We're going to Paris.'

'I'd love to go to Paris. You haven't been to Paris with me.'

'We will. In the spring sometime. Or Leiden, I have to go to Leiden for work, we could go there.'

'Leiden! Isn't that Holland or somewhere? Why would I want to go there? It's not exactly Paris, is it.'

'No, but it's a beautiful little—'

'OK. I get it. You and Mark. Paris. I hope you have a fantastic romantic time.'

The emotional blackmail became so intense I was on the point of asking Mark if he'd mind my going with her instead of him. I rehearsed in my mind what I'd say to him, and it sounded so feeble I dropped the idea. I thought about cancelling the trip altogether. Then I felt so resentful at Rachel for putting me on the spot I decided to go ahead with it.

In early December, Mark and I set off for our long weekend on the Left Bank. We stayed in a cheap hotel near the Luxembourg Gardens. I teased him about the bowl of water incident of his last trip to Paris. He remembered it as an epic adventure, to be embellished at every retelling.

On the Saturday afternoon we walked down to the Seine. It was bitterly cold, with a fine wintry drizzle. We could hear the rhythmic chanting and whistle-blowing of a demonstration, and near the Boulevard Saint Michel we caught up with it – hundreds of earnest students raging against some iniquity or other. Mark was all for joining in, and I tagged along. Soon he was quizzing a pretty young woman with wild red hair about the aims of the march. The authorities were trying to make university entrance more selective, she said: an outrage. I lagged behind, not wishing to cramp Mark's style; he was, yet again, between partners. At Odéon the column of demonstrators split. We found ourselves carried along by the press of bodies up to Place de la Sorbonne and into the university courtyard that I knew so well from my undergraduate year abroad, back in the early eighties.

Mark worked his way nearer the front, following the flame-haired young woman, while I skulked on the fringes. Speakers addressed the crowd. There was cheering, more chanting. And then a nervousness rippled through the assembly. The speaker halted in mid-sentence and asked what was happening. I could hear a drumming of truncheons on shields, and the thud of heavy boots. The riot police, the CRS, erupted into the courtyard, bellowing. Like sharks around a ball of baitfish, they forced the students into a compact mass, and there were panicky waves of movement back and forth as people tried to escape. The police brandished their truncheons and set about the demonstrators.

I'd lost sight of Mark in the chaos. When I spotted him, he was standing square on to a policeman, one arm shielding the pretty redhead. He was shouting abuse at the *flic*, who raised his truncheon. Mark tried to move back. I was screaming at him to get the hell out of there. But another surge of the crowd blocked him from view again.

I edged towards the northern end of the courtyard until I reached the entrance leading to the amphitheatres. I hurried inside, ran along a corridor, stopped, retraced my steps. I was close to panic as the shouts of the CRS reached me and my eyes started to water from the tear gas. My heart was thudding, I wanted to hare off in any direction, I couldn't think straight. I was, yes, very scared. But I was at a spot I recognised: the entrance to one of the grand amphitheatres, with its glass-panelled double doors. Something about its instant familiarity made my rational brain kick in. I knew this place, knew it well, from my student days. Throughout that year, I'd attended lectures at the Sorbonne, on nineteenth-century French literature. Every lunchtime I'd take a short cut from the lecture theatre to the rue Saint Jacques. You went down one of the long marbled corridors, *galéries* they called them, and turned right. Breaking the long corridor wall there was, I remembered, a little flight of steps down, with iron railings. And there was a short passageway, painted a dreary ochre and smelling of garbage. And at the end of the passageway, a door to the street.

Now, following a vestigial muscle memory of the route, I sprinted along the corridor, still panting and terrified but no longer aimless. At the end, I turned right. And there was the little flight of half a dozen steps leading down, just as I'd remembered. Grasping the iron rail, I jumped the stairs. I ran along the passage to the unassuming service door, pulled it. It opened. I rushed out into the rue Saint Jacques, hardly daring to believe I was safe. As I crossed the road, I saw a group of riot police beetling towards the door to block the escape of those coming after me.

I felt exhilaration, but it soon gave way to anxiety: where was Mark?

For hours I prowled the area looking for him, fearful at the charges of the CRS. I abandoned the search as darkness was falling, my eyes still streaming from the tear gas, my head aching. Fires flickered around me. Near the rue de Grenelle, a Honda of the police motorcycle brigade rode past, the driver revving the engine and mounting the pavement at speed to scatter pedestrians. The cop riding pillion stood up on the footrests, lashing out at fleeing students with his long truncheon.

I went back to the hotel and up to my room, rehearsing in my mind what I would say to Mark's parents back in London. But around ten o'clock he stomped in, muttering, 'Bastards! *Bastards!*' Below his bloodshot right eye was a deep red welt. His hair was matted with blood, his clothes were torn and filthy.

'Rifle butts, boots, truncheons, the works. The ones on motorbikes were the worst. But hey, you're all right, man, that's something.'

He relaxed enough to admit that it probably hadn't been a good idea to tell that *flic* in the Sorbonne courtyard that he was a fucking *conasse* who should go and fuck himself.

I told him about my escape.

'Epic, man,' he said. 'I wish I'd stayed with you.'

'I shouldn't have run off without you.'

'I'd have done the same. Live to fight another day.' He broke into a grin. 'Anyhow, I got her number. They slammed us in the same police van together. Cool chick!'

I wondered if he wasn't getting a bit old for such antics.

84

'You wouldn't possibly be jealous that I'm still having fun?'

'Who says *I'm* not having fun?' I said, lamely.

'Fun is an alien concept to you, cuz.' He slapped me on the shoulder to show the comment was not to be taken harshly, and with that he lay on the bed in his filthy clothes and fell asleep.

I picked up the phone. It wasn't too late to call Rachel. Her familiar voice soothed me. 'Enjoying yourselves, then?'

'Yeah,' I said. 'Got in a bit of a scrape today actually.'

'Oh?'

I told her briefly about the Sorbonne events, downplaying my terror, exaggerating the thrill of the escape, omitting my guilt at abandoning Mark.

'I'm not sure I like the sound of that.' She sighed. 'Do be careful, the pair of you.'

'I'll bring you with me the next time I go away. Just the two of us. Leiden. We'll go in spring, when the weather's better, I'll show you my old haunts.'

'Leiden. Hmm.'

'But Leiden's wonderful. A crime wave in Leiden means someone's nicked your bike. And it has fantastic botanical gardens.'

'But don't think I'm not coming with you to Paris as well...'

When I put the phone down I felt calmer. Then I started to worry that she'd resume her campaign to move to a bigger place in the new year, that she'd be choosing shower curtains and bed linen. And I thought that probably I shouldn't have phoned, shouldn't have mentioned Leiden. I needed to go there for work, to do some research on a horticulturalist called Clusius who'd been big in the sixteenth century in introducing tulips to the Dutch. Someone had written a fat historical novel about him, and the publisher had approached me to do the translation. I needed the work, tedious though the novel was. I'd be delving in the archives of the natural sciences department of the university. It would be difficult to take Rachel with me to meetings, she'd only get in the way. But if I didn't take her, she'd complain I was abandoning her.

Back in London, I tried to wriggle out of it. 'I'll be working all the time. You'll be bored,' I said.

'No I won't, I'll be fine. I love canals and windmills. And cheese with red rind. And I want to see the botanical gardens you're always going on about.'

We went to Leiden in April. It rained almost non-stop. We stayed in a shabby hotel near the university. On the second day, she claimed she saw a mouse in the room.

'It was probably only a cockroach,' I said, and next thing I knew, she was in tears.

'Why are you being so horrible to me? I hate this place.'

'I did tell you I'd have to go to meetings...'

'Yes, but you didn't tell me there'd be rats in the room and it rains the whole fucking time, and you ignore me when you *are* around...'

She shrugged off my comforting arm.

'What?' I said, irritated.

'I thought we'd have time to talk properly.'

'What is it you want to talk about?'

I knew the answer: she wanted to discuss renting somewhere together, how it would need to have a garden and a spare room for a baby or babies. She wanted to talk about the making of babies, her and me. She wanted to talk about my neglect of her, my disengagement. Now, she stared at me with scorn and exasperation, and turned her back.

'OK,' I said, 'Let's talk.'

'I can see it's pointless.'

She pulled down the blinds and took to her bed with painkillers, and sulked. Suddenly, I'd had enough. I wanted to be shot of her. *When we get back to London, I'll tell her we're finished,* I thought.

But events overtook us. On the Saturday, I had a free

morning and there was a gap in the clouds. I suggested we go to the Hortus Botanicus. It was one of the oldest botanical gardens in Europe. Rachel loved plants, was always talking about getting a garden, or an allotment. She made a show of reluctance but I could see she wanted to go.

It seemed OK at first. We entered the High Glasshouse, and scaled the steel staircase to the top walkway. She was fascinated by some dull bromeliads and succulents. 'I wonder if they sell plants. Or maybe I could just...'

I said, 'Look, I'm going on ahead, there's something I really want to see. Why don't you take your time with these things, have a good nose around, ask about cuttings. And join me in the Victoria greenhouse, it's marked on the little map. Say in fifteen minutes?'

She seemed disappointed. She wanted me with her, but she wanted to linger among the bromeliads even more. 'Can't you wait?' she asked. 'I won't be that long.'

'I know you, you'll get stuck here.'

'Honestly, couldn't we do something together, for once?'

'I'll see you there, OK.'

'Fine. Whatever.'

I went down to ground level and made for the complex of linked tropical greenhouses. The map wasn't all that clear, but I found it: the Victoria Amazonica, the world's largest water lily, in its own gallery. I'd last been to the Hortus Botanicus as a little kid with my parents, thirty-odd years earlier, but the lilies were still vivid in my mind. And here they were, as grotesque and fascinating as I'd remembered them. The enormous floating leaves were a metre or more across, flat with a vertical rim that made them seem like green-tinged metallic artefacts, not something organic. Away from the leaves, in its own patch of water, was the fruit, brownish and jagged, dangerous-looking, like a bear trap that might spring shut on a trailing limb. My mother's words on that first visit all those years before came to my mind. 'When it's ready it flowers, and the flowers are white the first night and the second night they turn pink.' I recalled clearly that to my young mind (I would have been six or so), this had seemed unsettling, the stuff of science fiction and nightmares. The lily was pollinated by some scarab, and this too seemed sinister, evoking visions of Pharaohs' tombs and crumbling mummies.

I was still thinking about all this when the door to the greenhouse opened and Rachel appeared, sweaty and cross.

'Didn't you think to come to look for me?' she said.

'Why, what's the matter?'

'I couldn't find the place. God!'

'It's on the little map.'

'That's no use, I've been going round in circles for the last half hour. What does "Jeen Ootgang" mean anyway?'

'*Geen uitgang*? No exit.'

'Why can't they write it in English! All those bloody plastic flaps. You might have at least tried to find me.'

'I didn't know you were lost.'

'I'm half an hour late in case you hadn't noticed.'

I hadn't noticed. I'd been thoroughly absorbed in the sight of these giant lily pads, and my childhood memories.

'What do you think of them?' I asked.

Rachel huffed and looked at the pond and the great floating leaves. 'I've no idea. What am I supposed to think about them?'

'They can be two metres across, they can take the weight of a baby.'

'What would anybody be doing putting a baby...?'

'All the Leidenaars used to come here to have their babies photographed on a big water-lily leaf, you go into people's homes here and sooner or later they drag out the photo of themselves or their parents or grandparents—'

'That's fine for those who have babies,' she said.

She turned away from me and the pond, arms folded,

and affected to look at the other plants in the gallery.

I sighed, repentant but also irritated. 'Look. Rachel. We can talk about it.'

She turned to face me again, fists clenched at her sides. 'No. We can't. We can never talk about it. *You* can never talk about it.'

'That's not true.'

'You're so wrapped up in all your translations and your bloody research, but what about the outside world? Doesn't it register with you at all? I may not be as brainy as you, but at least I do something useful in life.'

'Yeah, you do, but I don't think what I do is—'

'Christ, sometimes intelligent people can be so fucking dumb.'

'Look, I'm not sure where all this is coming from.'

'You don't want to have babies with me, do you?'

I stood silent.

'But you don't have the guts to come out with it. Well you don't, do you.'

And when I still said nothing, she burst into tears and ran towards an exit. Unfortunately it turned out to be '*geen uitgang*', and she retreated, thrusting away the thick hanging strips of translucent plastic, shaking her head and muttering, 'Oh for fuck's sake, this place!'

When I got back to the hotel, she and her bag had gone. She'd left a note, curt and final, and I breathed a sigh of relief. I saw her at the airport two days later. She wouldn't speak to me. We sat next to each other for the whole flight in uncomfortable silence. In the arrivals area at Heathrow, she left without saying another word.

I say I felt relief. But as the years slipped by and I saw liaisons come and go, I began to wonder if I was too old to settle down, have kids, if I'd missed the boat. In the earlier days of our relationship, when she could still be flip about things, Rachel would say, 'Your translations are your children, aren't they?'

And I'd say, 'Don't be ridiculous, they're far more

important than that.'

It's possible I really believed that then. She'd laugh, and her soft, puppyish brown eyes would tear up a little, and we'd move on to other things.

# Muito muito Inglês

My colleague Ana Ortega was flapping a hand in front of her face, trying to create a draught in the crowded foyer. The air conditioning had packed up in the main conference auditorium.

'Another session in there, in that heat, and people will be going into heart failure.'

'To die in Madrid?' I said.

Ana smiled, but barely. She blew a strand of hair off her forehead, and I wiped my own brow. She was an academic at the Universidad Complutense. A lot younger than me, but dynamic, competent, easy to work with. We'd teamed up following the publication of my translation of Roberto Tunsch's magisterially barmy *Malign Fragments*, which had got me a part-time university job in London, and invitations to contribute to academic debates. Ana was an expert on translating Irish literature into Spanish. She and I were co-editing a volume called *Changing Places: The new literary translation in Europe*, which involved trying to manage the unmanageable: a disunited Europe of individualistic academics. As Ana put it, in her Irish-inflected English, the task was 'like herding weasels at the crossroads'.

At the margins of my vision I was aware of a figure coming straight through the throng of delegates. A woman, cool and tanned in a white frock, stopped in front of us. She stood in a combative pose, head thrusting forwards.

'So you've ruined my chapter. It's now an incoherent mess. You think you know better?' She was nodding, as if in agreement with herself. 'So I'm the actual fucking expert here.' She hadn't raised her voice; there had been just the *pht-pht-pht* of her emphatic words.

I stared at her, my mouth dry. I hadn't recognised her at first sight, but that dangerous tone was unmistakeable: Julia Pinto Hughes. She was a couple of decades older than when I'd last seen her. Still slim, and with more authority. Her once long hair was shorter, darker, with blonde highlights. Her face was more lined. The eyes, though, were just as mean and calculating, and now glinting with toxic determination.

'Ana, this is Professor Pinto Hughes, author of the Portuguese chapter. Julia – Dr Ana Ortega.'

Ana held out her hand. Julia ignored it. Ana instinctively crossed her arms over her chest.

'You've made a mess of my chapter between you. I expected you to proofread it, not to do a total fucking rewrite. What were you thinking? It's an outrage.'

'We sent you our comments two weeks ago,' I managed to say. 'But we heard nothing back, so—'

'I can't be dealing with time-wasters, I was under the impression this would be a serious project.'

'It is.' People were glancing in our direction. 'Look, why don't we go somewhere quieter to discuss it,' I said.

'There's nothing to discuss.'

'I'm sorry, but there's plenty,' I said, miffed by her tone.

'Just pay us the courtesy of hearing us out,' Ana said.

'*Courtesy?*' Again a flashback to when I first knew her, still in our twenties: already she'd mastered the art of stripping a word of its innocence; of weaponising it.

Ana was businesslike and firm. 'Please, Professor Pinto, this way,' and she turned and walked towards a swing door. Julia huffed, but to my surprise she followed Ana. We filed along a corridor and found a seminar room that was at least not in direct sunshine.

We sat. Julia was unsmiling. Despite the stuffy heat, she seemed to radiate chill. She was the human equivalent of Kurt Vonnegut's ice-nine, a form of water that freezes anything that comes in contact with it.

'I'm not here to discuss or negotiate,' she said.

No academic chit-chat. No catch-up on the years since I'd last seen her. No acknowledgement even of our previous acquaintance.

'So,' I said, trying to keep my tone neutral, 'you have issues with our edits?'

'Your changes are totally unacceptable.'

'By which you mean—'

'That's fine, Professor Pinto,' Ana cut in, 'we can talk them through.'

'No. There's nothing to talk through. I made that clear.' There was a silence. Julia was looking down, as if inspecting the red varnish on her nails. She looked up again and said, 'You will restore my original version.'

'Excuse me?'

'You'll reverse your changes and restore my original.'

I shook my head. 'Julia, we're the editors. Editing the chapters is what we do. It's our job.'

'It's the process we're going through with all contributors.' Ana's voice was calm but her English accent had become less Irish (she'd studied at Trinity College Dublin), more Spanish-sounding.

'I'm sure you are.' Julia made it sound like an accusation.

'Yes. It's a matter of seeing that the same boxes are ticked, covering the themes. Trying to get consistency across the volume.'

'So the other chapters all came back covered in inane scrawls? On every page?'

'It varied,' said Ana. 'Some yes, others not so much.'

'So what you're saying is that my draft was substandard?'

'There were some issues, but we expect that in a first draft.'

'Yes,' I echoed. 'There were problems with it. That needed fixing.'

'I think what we mean is that we went through a process with all the authors,' Ana said.

'Yes, regardless of whether—'

'I can't believe I'm hearing this. I'm an expert of international standing, I'm not some fucking first-year doctoral student.'

'Yes,' said Ana. 'We appreciate that.'

'I wouldn't have agreed to take part had I known what I'd be dealing with.'

I wanted to shout: *Agreed to take part? When it was you who muscled your way into the project to begin with. Because you thought it would be bad for your image if someone else wrote the chapter on Portugal.* But I stayed silent. Through my mind went the ditty that subversive colleagues were said to recite when rolled over by this woman: *Who could ever refuse/Julia Pinto Hughes?*

'OK Julia,' Ana was saying, 'we will need to take some time out to consider your request and we'll get back—'

'So it's very simple,' said Julia. 'You restore my version in full, with the exception of the line edits for typos and for house style. Or I withdraw from the project.'

'But Julia, you're going to wreck the whole volume,' I blurted out. I could have kicked myself for my stupidity.

'You're accusing me of sabotage?' Her ice-nine voice conjured up a scenario of official letters of complaint to my dean and vice-chancellor, a phalanx of libel lawyers. Unlikely, maybe, but you never knew with Julia Pinto Hughes.

'I want a response by close of play today. The ball's in your court.' She got up and walked out of the room, leaving the door open.

We heard her click along the corridor on her heels.

'Bloody Julia!' I shouted as the sound faded. Ana, after an initial cry of exasperation, sat quietly, letting me rant.

'Why did we ever let ourselves be bullied into having her on the project? We shouldn't have let her anywhere near it...'

Ana murmured soothingly, waiting for my frustration blow itself out.

'... And then she comes up with such a mediocre chapter, Christ, a first-year undergraduate would have been embarrassed to hand that in.'

'Perhaps we should think of how to rescue the situation.'

I ignored Ana's sensible suggestion. 'She might have

made an effort to address the themes of the book. Half the references are to her own bloody publications. We should have shown more backbone, damn it. I've half a mind to run after her and tell her not to be such a prima donna.'

Ana smiled. 'Probably not a good idea.'

I slumped in the chair, defeated. 'OK. What now? What are we going to do? Apologise, eat humble pie? Gently offer some suggestions to make the chapter stronger?'

'If you think that's the best option.'

'Well it's that or...' I trailed off.

Ana was staring out of the window, pushing a fingertip down on the sharp point of a pencil which she revolved with the finger and thumb of her other hand, back and forth, back and forth. She put the pencil down and looked at the small depression in the flesh of her fingertip. There was a hardness in Ana's gaze that I'd not suspected her capable of. 'We could thank her for her participation and accept her resignation from the project.'

'What?' I said. 'Like, *Eff off back to London, Julia?*' I felt a brief euphoria at the prospect of resistance. 'Would love to. But it wouldn't work. We can't *not* have a chapter on Portugal and it's too late to get someone else to do it.'

Ana puckered her lips as if considering something. 'So we write the chapter ourselves.'

'Us? You and me? What do we know about the Portuguese translation scene?'

'Quite a lot. I've translated dos Santos into Spanish, and you and I can both read Portuguese.'

'I guess we'd do a better job than Julia with the secondary sources. But will the chapter have any credibility? We're not experts.'

'We could ask a Portuguese colleague to take a look at our draft and give us comments.'

I blew out air. 'What? Someone like Vítor Céu Andrade at Coimbra? I guess it might work.'

'Coimbra? Isn't that where Julia is a visiting professor?'

'I think it is, yes. But he's an expert on the Portuguese

translation scene. Unless you've got a better idea.'

'No,' she said. She sucked at the black mark on her finger where the pencil had been. 'OK, let's try it.'

We sat in silence for while, digesting the implications of the plan.

'What about the publishing editor?' I said. 'She's a friend of Julia's.'

'That was the first time I've met Julia, but it strikes me she doesn't have friends. She's the sort of person who has allies, and people who owe her favours.'

This was true. Many people were afraid of her, or held her in awe for her (rather tin-eared, in my opinion) translations of pioneering Brazilian feminist writers like Alma Sertão. But no one actually liked her.

Ana said, 'I could have a quiet word with the publisher. They've invested quite heavily in us and won't want to pull out.'

'Good. I'll ring Vítor. Though maybe we should sleep on it, have another conversation with Julia.'

'I'm not having another conversation with that woman.' She seemed energised by her instinctive antipathy to Julia.

When we got back to the conference room, the air conditioning was working and Julia had left. That evening I phoned Vítor and he agreed to help.

\*\*\*

By the end of November, we had the first draft of a chapter on literary translation in Portugal. I emailed it to Vítor. He was a well-known translator and academic, and a bookish man. We were old acquaintances, brought close by our shared passion for translating the obscurer works of the Peruvian novelist José María Arguedas. He'd just finished his Portuguese version of Arguedas's prison novel, *El Sexto* – the same book I had worked on for so many years – and had found a Lisbon publisher keen to take it on.

A week later, his comments on our chapter came back.

The draft was littered with 'track changes' and marginal notes about our misreadings and crass errors. Vítor was in London and wanted to talk things through with me. We met at a gallery café on the South Bank, overlooking the river. He greeted me warmly and complained about the execrable coffee, almost as a ritual, knowing it amused me.

'Ana and I are so grateful for what you've done, Vítor.'

'At least,' he said, in his excellent English with its slight foreign inflection, the sibilant esses, 'it is better than anything she would have come up with, right!'

'You think so?'

'Definitely.' After a beat he added, with a southern European shrug and accompanying gesture of his hands, *'But...'*

'But what?'

He smiled and rocked his head from side to side, conveying an indefinable reservation. At last he said, 'Well, how shall I put this? I think it is still, you know, *muito muito inglês.'*

'Too English? Is that a bad thing?'

'Yes,' he said. 'It's too definite, too black and white, not subtle, not nuanced enough, not enough room for interpretation and alternative readings. Things are never so simple.'

'Ah,' I responded. 'Too Julia-esque?'

'Maybe. Yes, perhaps. *Muito júliaesco!'*

He chuckled, and his chuckle became a full-throated laugh. I laughed too, feeling warm towards him and his wry, generous humour. But then he pulled a face, twisting his mouth and sucking in a hard breath, as if wincing in pain. I caught myself wincing too. Perhaps we already intuited the prospect of a Julia-esque response.

\*\*\*

I next saw Vítor a year or so later, that would be 2010 I guess, at a conference in Paris on the Latin American translation boom. We hadn't been in touch since the chapter had been wrapped up. The book was now out, and I'd brought with me a hardback copy that Ana and I had inscribed for him. Vítor and I embraced, exchanged backslaps and disengaged. He looked me in the eyes and took hold of my forearms. I felt mildly uncomfortable.

'How are you?' he said.

'I wish I had a bit more work. All these young translators, fresh off their courses, hungry to make a mark, undercutting our rates... But, you know, can't complain.'

'As you English always say!'

'Look, I have something for you.'

I took the book out of my briefcase and held it out to him. He accepted it without saying anything, just glanced at the austere academic cover. I noticed how world-weary he looked, his jowly, hang-dog face even more dragged down than usual, his brown eyes more protuberant. The large brownish-pink mole in the middle of his forehead seemed to have become larger and more spherical to the point where it was distracting.

'We were so grateful for the way you helped us out,' I said. 'Would have been tricky without you. Anyway, how are things?'

'Oh, you know. "Can't complain"!'

His expression was half wan smile, half pained grimace. 'E...'

'What is it, Vítor?'

'I should never have agreed to help you.'

'Don't say that.'

'It is true, sadly. But it's OK. It's just the way it is.'

'The way *what* is?'

'News got out. I don't know how. Perhaps she made certain *deductions*. In her eyes, I'm guilty. And so are you, of course.'

'I don't get it. It's not as if you actually wrote the chapter. Yes, you did give us some very helpful pointers, without which we would probably have disgraced ourselves. But we are responsible for it, not you.'

'Maybe. But I paid the price. After she got to hear that I'd helped you...' He stopped for a moment. When he resumed, his voice was shaky. He wouldn't look at me. 'Well, I was purged, I became a non-person. I didn't get my promotion, can't move universities. I'm imprisoned, she is my jailer.'

'But that's appalling.'

'Of course.'

'Christ! I'm so sorry, Vítor, I had no idea. Is there anything I can do? There must be something. I could...' I was fantasising about phoning Julia, we'd have a blazing row, I'd accuse her of malice and petty-mindedness, of abuse of power. The prospect of confronting her terrified me.

'No! No, my friend,' said Vítor. 'Anything you tried would make it worse. She has already blocked publication of my Arguedas translation – she knows the publisher, she will have had a quiet word with him. All that wasted effort.'

'That's outrageous!'

'Yes. But she's a powerful woman. And she is *vingativa*. How do you say it – vengeful?'

I had a glimpse into a troubling parallel world, where the logic was not my logic, where cause and effect were mysterious and opaque, the meaning of things always just beyond reach.

'But how can you be sure it's all because of her?'

'One can never be sure. But, you know, she's a visiting professor at my university... That's how things work. Quiet words. Winks and nods.'

'So you have actual evidence that she—'

'Evidence!'

Vítor gave a short, caustic laugh, as if the question were stupid, *muito muito inglês*.

## PINTO HUGHES HAS KINDLY AGREED

I met Roberto Tunsch once, back in 2001. It was like an audience with an ageing rock star. The author of *Fragmentos malintencionados* sat in his hotel room in Buenos Aires, hair white and magnificently unkempt, a goatee beard like that of a Velázquez royal. The great man was elusive, playful, giving one-word answers to my nervous, earnest questions, or going on at length about topics I wasn't interested in.

*Fragmentos* is a modern Paraguayan masterpiece or a pile of pretentious garbage, according to taste. I tend to the former view, probably because its publication in English led to my belated breakthrough (such as it was) as a literary translator. The novel has an absurdly convoluted plot. Silver deposits are found beneath Capitol Hill in Washington. A ruined palace belonging to a kleptomaniac post-Communist ruler figures prominently. The hero is a Lebanese-Paraguayan called Adolfo Tarir Espósito who uses his fearsome halitosis as a weapon to humiliate and dominate. Tunsch will spend fifty pages describing the nature and philosophy of bad breath and volatile sulphur compounds, and what the effect is on the observer. But his subversive humour keeps you going through the marshier passages. So, he puts in a plug for a real mouthwash, called Resulfexx, then recounts how he went to Procter & Gamble and asked for money for this blatant product placement and tells us exactly what their response was. (He reproduces their emails to him verbatim.)

Tunsch's style makes life difficult for the translator. For example, the sound and feeling of chemical terms in Spanish is so different from their recondite dryness in English. He lapses frequently into Paraguayan slang, and peppers the text with ambiguous phrases in the indigenous Guaraní language. I aimed for something seamless, flowing. I think I did quite well in the end, but it was a struggle.

There's also the constant wordplay and punning. What should you do with a snatch of dialogue like, '*Le llamé a Teo*' (I called/phoned Theo)? For the listener, it could be heard as '*Le llamé ateo*' (I called him/her/you an atheist), which in Jesuitical Paraguay could be a weighty accusation. The surreptitious, almost subliminal allusions to popular culture are even worse, because they're often so hard to spot. Tunsch sneaks in dozens of phrases that are quotations from popular tangos by Gardel, or poems by the melancholy master of the pampas ballad, José Larralde: *qué mano tronchó tu suerte?/tal vez la mano del tiempo*. By whose hand was your fate sealed?/Perhaps by the hand of time... I had to try to come up with equally unobtrusive equivalents that would be meaningful to a British or – more importantly – American readership: recognisable but not glaringly obvious phrases from the lyrics of Frank Sinatra songs perhaps, or from Bob Dylan, or John Lennon.

When I went to see Tunsch, I gave him a list of the allusions I'd identified in *Fragmentos*. Smiling, he refused to confirm or deny that the list was either definitive or accurate. 'Translation,' he said, 'is reinvention. There are a thousand ways to stay true to the original.' So I was working in the dark, always worried that I was missing something. I hoped readers wouldn't notice all the hard labour that went into the English version. Though, equally, a part of me wanted them to realise it wasn't as easy as it looked.

Anyway, after *Fragments* came out I quite quickly became, if not a celebrity of the translation world, at least fairly well known. I started getting invitations to give talks at book festivals in the UK and abroad, and to coordinate edited volumes like the one with Ana Ortega. I spoke at the Círculo de Bellas Artes in Madrid, at the Academiegebouw of the University of Leiden, at the Cercle de Traducteurs de Montréal. Young translators would email me out of the blue for advice, or ask for my Twitter handle (I didn't have one). And I no longer had to hustle so hard for commissions. Publishers often came to me, though the pay was still miserly and the books dreary. Several years after the publication of *Fragments*, it was still the work I was best known for. One spring, 2011 or 2012 I think, I received an official-looking letter from the Universidad de Navarra inviting me to give a plenary address at a glitzy event in San Sebastián in northern Spain. The theme of the gathering was *Latin American Literature: To Foreignise or to Domesticate?* At the time I was working on a translation of Tunsch's essays, which were as playful, allusive and frustrating as his novels. I thought I'd leave the academic stuff to the academics, and give a light, witty talk on the challenges and delights of translating an author like Tunsch.

\*\*\*

At the registration, the organisers greeted me with a deference that still felt misplaced, undeserved. I was drinking mint tea, looking round for some real mint leaves to add some bite and depth to the musty teabag, when Ana Ortega arrived. The collection of essays we'd co-edited on new approaches to literary translation in Europe had been well received. Working with someone so calm and competent had been one of the consolations of a difficult venture. Ana was originally from San Sebastián, and still had family there, so I was hoping she might show me around away from the tourist hotspots. We greeted each other warmly, and were chatting about the pleasures of the town, when I received my first intimation of gathering disaster. A young man came up to me, scrutinised my name badge and gave a sneer as if to say, 'thought as much'.

'Who the hell was that?' I asked as he walked away.

'Probably one of Julia Pinto Hughes' young Turks,' Ana said.

103

'Ana, that's not funny.'

Julia Pinto Hughes was, of course, an old adversary. A woman so ruthlessly self-serving that powerful men were said to climb out of ground-floor office windows to avoid her. A woman who'd almost sunk our edited collection of essays, and who'd tried to destroy the career of a colleague who'd dared to help us. And, as it happened, a woman with whom I'd only just failed to have a one-night stand a quarter of a century earlier.

'Don't worry,' said Ana, 'she's not going to attack you with her stiletto heels in a public place.'

'Who knows?'

'No, she'll wait until she gets you alone on a dark corridor.'

Ana turned out to be wrong about that.

I walked back along the sea front from the conference venue to my hotel. They'd put me in one of those luxurious places overlooking the famous curving beach, la Contxa. It was more like a film set than a real place. My hotel room was large: a king-size bed, a sofa, an enormous television, a writing desk covered in green leather, a terrace overlooking the bay. I went through my plenary address to the conference. I'd called it *The Deadly Serious Playfulness of Roberto Tunsch*. I was pleased with the title: neatly oxymoronic, capturing the essence of the man, of the writer, signalling the trickiness of translating him. Titles are important, they shape expectations, guide the audience through the thickets of the argument.

I stood in front of the mirror for a rehearsal. I've never really liked the sight of myself in a mirror: a little hunched, furtive, as if caught in the act of looking for an escape route. Maybe I don't come across like that when I'm talking to someone, engaging, smiling, listening. I don't know, I hope not. I read the speech aloud. Forty minutes, closely argued but leavened with jokes; I thought my enthusiasm for Tunsch came through.

Outside, on the promenade, the light was fading, and

people were gathering to stroll and display themselves.

*\*\*\**

I still see it all very clearly. I see myself walking to the front of the auditorium, feeling self-conscious, setting down my files on the table next to the lectern; quite a few people already in the tiered seats, and more coming in. And there she was. Julia Pinto Hughes. Of course she was, she was always going to be there. And she probably had an additional grudge now, because it was me rather than her giving the keynote address.

I registered how overheated and stuffy it was. My eyes wanted to screw up tight against the glare of the spotlights. The place had filled, and there was that familiar expectant hum, so intimidating to the speaker. I was massaging my eyes with the heels of my hands. The chairman, Frank Vallejo, was sitting next to me, and next to him was a chair for the discussant. Vallejo put his hand on my shoulder and murmured, 'There's been a late change to the programme. D'Onofrio is ill.'

'Oh?'

'Yes. Professor Pinto Hughes has kindly agreed to step in as discussant at short notice.'

I could feel my jaw working, my molars clamping together.

Vallejo said, 'Tried to contact you last night, but it was quite late, so…'

Julia was just taking her seat to my right. I caught her eye, and she nodded with an expression that seemed to say, *Well, there you are, fate has presented me with a chance to screw you.* Our last encounter had been so unpleasant, that clash over her contribution to the edited volume of essays. Knowing Julia, she would have been up all night, speed-reading my translation, comparing it with the original, planning her line of attack.

Vallejo was introducing me as a distinguished translator

from Spanish and Dutch. I was relieved to see Ana Ortega in the second row. She smiled and gave me a little nod of encouragement.

I heard myself begin. I was sounding steady. I tried to breathe evenly, got through the section about Tunsch's place in the Latin American canon, the inevitable comparisons with Roa Bastos.

'If you were to mix Benedetti's morose optimism with César Aira's inconsequential non sequiturs and add a pinch of Bioy Casares' low-key menace with a just hint of Saer's existential musings,' I said, 'Roberto Tunsch is what you'd get.'

I was surprised by an unexpected noise: the sound of knowledgeable listeners chuckling in appreciation. I relaxed a little, the spasms in my eye muscles were gone, and I dared to gaze out over the audience. I cracked a lame joke about boom and bust in literary translation. There was another ripple of laughter.

I was into a passage about hidden popular music references in *Fragmentos* and how culture-savvy students had helped me find appropriate equivalents in English. The chair was leaning back. Out of the corner of my eye I could see Julia Pinto Hughes shaking her head and smiling faintly, as if amused by the wrongness of my argument. I might even have imagined it. But the strain was back in my voice.

In my peripheral vision I sensed Julia's manicured hands stretching out on the table in front of her. She seemed to be examining the trademark blood-red of her painted nails. I was aware of her holding each finger in turn in the other hand and rubbing the nail deliberately with her thumb. I didn't know what the gesture meant, but it unnerved me. My mouth went dry and my throat tightened. I sipped from the glass of water, then again, and a third time. With each sip I felt the audience slip a little further. Don't look at her, I thought, just at your words on the page. But it was like a compulsion, my eyes kept jerking to the right. At last, the conclusion. And even as I was saying them, I knew those final phrases sounded banal; *were* banal.

The chair said a perfunctory thank you and introduced the discussant as a highly distinguished professor of comparative literature, a woman who'd brought the new generation of post-feminist Brazilian writers to an English-language readership.

Julia apologised for not being d'Onofrio. 'Sadly, he's unwell, a surfeit of San Sebastián's exquisite *pintxos*, I imagine,' she said, managing to be flattering and insulting in one breath. The audience laughed. Begging indulgence for having to speak off the cuff, Julia launched a systematic assault on my translation of Tunsch for its patriarchal deep structure. It was my turn to shake my head: it wasn't the job of the translator to make reparations for the political incorrectness of the author's original text. But among the audience, there were many nodding heads.

Julia claimed my translation had not only reproduced but compounded Tunsch's offence. Take, for example, my choice of Western analogues of Latin American popular music referenced in the original. 'One might have picked, let's say, Carole King, Joni Mitchell, Nina Simone. Even Beyoncé or Madonna. But no, he sticks safely to Bob Dylan, Woody Guthrie, Frank Sinatra, John Lennon. The dreary old pale male canon. A translator worth her salt might have "domesticated" the misogynistic slant of the original text for a western European sensibility. Instead of which he reproduces the "foreignness" of a profoundly patriarchal social order. Bravo! A masculinist tour de force.'

And so on. Her caustic message was reinforced rather than undercut by a relaxed, almost blithe delivery, and she had the audience in the palm of her hand. I could see Ana, still sitting quietly. A frown of concern had replaced her earlier smile.

Julia was going on about Augusto Monterroso. 'He wrote the shortest story in the Spanish language. I shall

107

read it to you in its entirety – don't worry, it's barely one line long: "*Cuando despertó, el dinosaurio todavía estaba allí.*"'

Oh, that awful Spanish accent, like a knife on a saucepan, just as bad as it was when we were postgraduate students of literary translation together in Lima in the 1980s.

'Now,' she continued, 'what happens when you translate such a sentence – and *Fragmentos* is full of them – into English? Well, Umberto Eco, that paragon of the polymathic, cultured (male) translator, gives us this: "When he woke up, the dinosaur was still there." At least half the audience will be aware of something not quite right here. The Spanish does not define the gender of the protagonist. "*Despertó*" can be rendered as either "he woke up" or "she woke up". Or even "it woke up". Thus Eco makes definite something that was indefinite, and does so in a way that reinforces a male perspective. And so it is with this translation of *Fragmentos*. At every turn, where the translator has the opportunity to keep the sense undetermined, he closes it down. And always, without exception, in a way that reinforces male dominance in the narrative.'

Julia was right. I'd translated the Spanish with a masculine pronoun wherever there was doubt, and had done so intuitively, without even thinking it through. Probably 'he' was the correct choice, but I'd never considered the alternative. I felt angry at myself for this oversight, and more angry at Julia for having pointed it out. Umberto Eco says translation is a negotiation between the original language and the target language. Not for Julia Pinto Hughes it wasn't. Translation was an act of gender warfare, in which I was the oppressor. Julia was one of nature's ultras, whose demands on the text and on those who handled the text were uncompromising and non-negotiable.

She was reaching her severe conclusion: 'Giuseppe

Tomasi di Lampedusa acknowledges the truth of all Conservatism: that for things to stay the same, they have to change. In this case, the translator by his conservative modifications to the text has acted as a bulwark of the male hegemony propounded by the deep structure of *Fragmentos*. "*Fragmentos malintencionados*" indeed: *malign* from beginning to end.' She stopped speaking to more enthusiastic applause than I had achieved as keynote speaker, and all over the auditorium hands shot into the air as Vallejo prepared to take questions.

I slumped in my chair, knowing that people were looking at me, fascinated or horrified by my discomfiture on the spotlit stage. Ana sat with her arms folded tight against her chest. Her hand had not shot up. Was she keeping her powder dry, biding her time, striking late? Or was she, perhaps, planning to back up Julia's onslaught? *No*, I thought, *she's caught in a bind. She wants to come to my defence, but she's seen as one of my people and anything she says would only make matters worse.* So she sat silent, squirming, while I fantasised that maybe she could, in a gender role reversal, be my knight in shining armour and come to my rescue, and... And, what, hoist me up with one elegant sweep of the arm onto the back of her steed and gallop away from the volley of arrows?

My attention snapped back to a questioner who was now on her feet. 'What would you say to the accusation that *Resulfexx* is emblematic of the deodorising effect of male power plays?'

After it was over, there was another curt nod from Julia, a thin smile. She was on her phone, those well-turned legs tightly crossed. She knew she was powerful enough to afford to show some thigh. She'd already moved on, I was yesterday's news. As I slunk out of the auditorium I had to put up with those slip-sliding, embarrassed looks of colleagues, their chit-chat about anything but the talk. I avoided the coffee lounge. I was just leaving the building when Ana caught up with me.

'Well done,' she said. 'You OK?'

'What do you mean "well done"? It was a disaster.'

'No it wasn't. The talk was very good. Well-structured. Julia was just on an ego trip.'

'But it's her comments people will take away from it, not my talk.'

'Come on. It's not that bad.' She put out a hand and touched my arm.

'I thought you might have asked a question,' I said. Instantly I regretted it.

'I wanted to ask something. But I couldn't think of anything sensible.' She made a caricature sad face, mouth turned down. 'I've never actually read any Tunsch.'

It seemed like a double betrayal. I said, 'Never mind, Ana. It doesn't matter.'

'You coming for lunch?'

'Er, no, thanks.'

She put an hand on my shoulder and kissed me on each cheek. As usual, she wore no scent, there was just the smell of fresh skin. 'Look, I'll catch you later,' she said. As she went back into the lobby, she called out, '*Cuídate.*' Look after yourself.

The afternoon was something of a blur. I walked along the promenade back to my hotel, went to my room. I tried to read, but couldn't concentrate, so I watched a mindless game show on Spanish television. I imagined lying on a sofa next to Ana, my head against her shoulder, her hand stroking my hair. *Cuídame tú*, I thought – you, Ana, look after me. I may have dozed. Later, I skulked down for an evening meal in the hotel restaurant. I ordered a bottle of wine. Ate, drank. Drank some more. Quite out of character, I started on a second bottle. The local white. Good if you like that sort of thing – *pétillant*.

I was finishing my seared tuna steak when Julia Pinto Hughes walked in with an entourage of male doctoral students. There were only two of them, but they behaved like an entourage. One of them was that young man who'd earlier sneered at my name badge. They smell power, these young people. And its absence. I was feeling quite pissed, and resentful and sorry for myself. I'd flopped, it was her bloody fault. Normally I'd avoid confrontation, but it must have been the bubbles in the wine. I'd drunk it too quickly and it had gone to my head. I was up out of my chair without having made a conscious decision.

Julia didn't look put out to see me looming at her, a little unsteady, flustered and angry.

'Julia,' I said.

'Hello,' she said, 'All right?'

'No, not all right.'

'OK, fair enough.' She smiled, unruffled. 'Quite a decent restaurant this, I hear.' She saw me sway. 'Can I get you a coffee or something?'

'I mean, after what you did to Vítor. And to me. Don't you dare... don't you dare try anything with Ana. I swear...'

'Excuse me?'

'You know full well. Vítor Céu Andrade. Blocked his book. Destroyed his career. And this afternoon, wow. Mine, as good as. Sabotaged. Fuck.'

'Well, I didn't sabotage you. Possibly you could have addressed the issues a bit more sharply, but it was quite a robust debate, I thought.'

I found myself deflated, having been pumped up for action.

'As for Vítor,' she continued, 'I'm not sure what exactly you think you know. If you mean his failure to get promotion, I had nothing to do with it.'

'You screwed him!' I shouted.

'You're making yourself ridiculous,' she said, calm but icy.

I was beginning to have a glimmer of doubt. 'I'm not ridiculous, what you did—'

'No, stop there. Not what I did.' Her chin was raised now, assertive. 'What Vítor did. He's very lucky he has a job at all. And it's nothing to do with the edited volume.'

'What!' I managed to sound both cross and confused.

She relaxed her aggressive posture and sighed. 'I'll order you a coffee.'

'What about them?' I said, ludicrously, waving at the two doctoral students.

She ignored me.

I said, 'I'd rather have a mint tea. Real mint leaves.'

She'd already caught a waiter's eye and had ordered aperitifs for the students and a strong black coffee for me.

My coffee arrived and she took it and led me out of the restaurant and across the road to the promenade. It was a warm evening, with a pleasant breeze. You could see the lights shimmering around the curve of the bay, the little wooded island just visible as a silhouette, the feathery branches of the trees black against the dying light to the west.

Julia lit a cigarette. I hadn't known she still smoked. In Lima she used to, we all used to.

She said, 'Vítor Céu Andrade demanded sexual favours of one of his female doctoral students and, it subsequently transpired, two other young women on the Masters programme. And as for blocking his book, it was the financial crisis that put paid to that—'

'Vítor demanding sexual favours? That's a lie,' I muttered, knowing as I said the words that the allegation had to be true.

'You can check it out, it's on the public record. Or ask him yourself. Lucky for him I wasn't on the disciplinary panel.'

My hands were shaking. I'd spilt some of my strong black coffee into the saucer. I looked out to sea.

'Fine view, isn't it?' she said.

I breathed out hard. She was standing close to me, leaning on the ornate cast-iron railings. I caught a waft of her perfume and thought of our younger selves in Lima, twenty, twenty-five years before, how we'd left a party together at dawn. How nothing had happened. Because an earthquake had happened.

'I'm sorry,' she said, 'I've got to get back to my young men.' She gave me an ironic look.

'Just lay off Ana Ortega.'

'Ana, eh?' She murmured, 'Ah! Ana,' as if for herself. 'I'm not sure what you think I might do to her, and in any case she seems more than capable of looking after herself.'

She took a last deep drag on her cigarette, and tossed it into the wind coming off the Bay of Biscay. She turned back to me. 'For what it's worth, I think it's a perfectly decent translation. Just not a very good book to begin with.'

I followed her back into the hotel, feeling unpleasantly sober. I made myself walk up the four flights of stairs to my room, irritated by the conversation. It had failed to show Julia in the worst possible light, and raised uncomfortable questions about Vítor. I switched on my laptop and did a search of his university, scanned the local Coimbra newspapers. Soon, I found it, a brief reference to a student complaint, a disciplinary panel in the department of literary translation, the university authorities' refusal to comment further.

It was still early. There was a knock at my bedroom door. I looked through the peephole. It was Ana, and I let her in.

'I just came to see how you were.'

'I'm fine. Fine. Come in, good to see you.' I realised I was blushing. Was it my last inane comment to Julia to leave Ana alone, and her enigmatic response of 'Ah! Ana'? Julia was right: I had no idea what I thought she might do to her.

'I'll put the kettle on,' I said.

'That would be nice.'

Ana perched on the edge of the king-size bed – presumably she thought the gesture would not be misconstrued – while I clumsily brewed the tea. I was thinking that, if I were fifteen years younger, I'd go for someone like Ana. Someone steady, good-looking in an unflashy way, who engaged you as an equal, with her understated strength and confidence. It made a woman attractive, an attractiveness that would have lasted even when looks had faded. I shook these fantasies from my mind. They were unseemly: I was not far off fifty; Ana was early thirties, thirty-five at most. I didn't even know for sure if she was gay or straight.

'Ah,' I said, 'I've just remembered.' I searched in my jacket pocket for a little plastic bag into which I'd placed a handful of mint leaves. I'd filched them from a bowl of fresh fruit salad on our table at the conference lunch. They were sad-looking, but I emptied them out into our cups on top of the mint teabags, and added the boiling water. Ana laughed and shook her head.

'You and your mint!'

She watched me sip at my tea. 'How do you feel?' she asked again.

I shrugged. 'A bit mauled.'

She said, 'It really wasn't that bad. Anyway, *Cosas que pasan en el campo.*'

I smiled. The things that go on in the countryside. Which means, roughly, *stuff happens*. It was a quote, more or less, from one of Larralde's songs.

'Yeah, I guess I'm OK.'

'Good. I think basically she's a bit jealous of your success and reputation.'

'Julia?'

'Uh-huh. She likes to be *out there*, doesn't she?'

I was surprised at the edge to Ana's tone. She really didn't like Julia. It was an opening for me to get my anger off my chest.

'Fucking Julia,' I said. 'She's always been a complete narcissist.'

Ana listened, nodding, murmuring the odd word of

114

comfort or agreement, blowing at her mint tea without drinking. At one point she leaned across and grasped my wrist in her hand and squeezed. She didn't say much, but managed to let me know that it was all right, that things would be OK.

'Do you think Julia has got a point, Ana? I mean about sexism and translation?'

'There's a point in there somewhere, yes. But she overstates the case. She's too dogmatic, she's an ideologue. Things are more complicated in the real world.' She paused before adding, 'I don't know, I'd have to read your translation to comment, wouldn't I?'

We grinned at each other.

'It's OK,' I said, 'I've forgiven you.'

'I hope so!'

When I'd exhausted myself on the subject of Julia, I said, 'Sorry, Ana. Enough of all that.'

'I don't mind at all, she'll get her just deserts one of these days.'

I nodded. I liked the way Ana used idiomatic but slightly dated phrases like 'just deserts'. Briefly I wondered what Julia's deserts might be, but my anger seemed to have run its course. We chatted a bit more about inconsequential things, and the conversation petered out.

'So,' she said, 'OK.'

I inquired, for form's sake, whether she'd like something stronger than tea. She declined with a smile, and got up.

'Thanks,' I said. 'I feel much better for talking to you.'

At the door, she laid a hand on my shoulder. It seemed to linger there for a moment longer than was necessary. The door clicked softly shut behind her. I turned and contemplated the enormous bed. I undressed and lay down, wide awake still, and folded my arms under my head. I tried not to think of Julia but of Ana, her watchful, calm face, her hand warm on my shoulder, her ability to soothe my wounded ego. Yes, Ana was right: my success,

115

my reputation were solid, Julia's grandstanding could not dent them. But I kept getting flashbacks to some of the sorrier moments of the talk, to Julia's eager assault, my fumbling attempts to defend myself.

Weary of it all I picked up the television remote control. At this time of night there seemed to be little on except for shabby little adverts for porn sites. I flicked through the channels for a few minutes before drifting off into a broken, uneasy sleep.

# Sex Instruction for Irish Farmers

The morning after my disastrous talk, I couldn't face the other conference delegates. I skipped breakfast and the morning session, and sneaked out of the hotel. At the edge of the town I took a steep wooded path leading to the little fishing village of Pasajes de San Juan. The day was bright and clear, and there was a smell of pine needles. By the time I got to Pasajes I was feeling better. But as I took the little ferry across the mouth of the port, and wandered from bar to bar for snacks and beers, I couldn't get Ana out of my head.

A dangerous idea began to form. Why not ask her directly if she was interested in me? I'd dreamed of her in the night. Though I didn't recall the details, the dream had a vague erotic atmosphere that lingered, making me think I'd crossed a professional boundary.

Maybe, I thought, we could get beyond collegiality, build something more. I found myself deep in one of those endless internal dialogues – the kind you hoped you'd grow out of after adolescence – in which your sane self tries to fend off your wheedling devil's advocate self.

And she might not be into men.

*She'll tell you.*

Yes, but coming on to a colleague could be seen as harassment. I'm not that guy.

*Not that guy? Or just don't have the guts?*

Of course I've got the guts.

*Like with Gabi? Bottled it.*

I didn't bottle it, the circumstances weren't right.

*Christ Almighty. The human race would have died out if all men were like you.*

Shut up.

*How about tonight?*

Erm, I've got a shocking hangover, and I'm... I'll wait till I'm back in London.

*No. Tonight.*
Ferfuckssake!
*Tonight it is.*
My sane, rational self knew exactly what she'd say. But there was something very persuasive about the idea of 'tonight', because it was the last night we'd all be together at the conference.

I walked back to town rather than taking the bus, hoping that the hike would be strenuous enough to stop me fantasising about Ana. But however hard I sweated and strained, however much I tried to take in the beauty of the sea views from the stony cliff-top path, her image kept coming back to me, calm, thoughtful, and now disturbingly eroticised.

I got to the conference and slumped at the back through the afternoon plenary. I couldn't concentrate. Ana wasn't there. That evening I caught sight of her at the conference dinner, at a table too far away even to wave. I wanted to go over to her, but I felt I'd be exposed to the mocking gaze of the curious. I wasn't ready for another public humiliation.

Dignitaries made the usual boring speeches. Afterwards, delegates hung around in the bar. There wasn't much of an atmosphere; people were mentally preparing to leave. No sign of Ana. I returned to my room to pack.

Around midnight I went to bed. My brain was still churning. I tried deep breathing but kept losing the rhythm as the thoughts intruded. A church clock struck half past the hour, then one o'clock, like a reproach. I got up and put on some clothes, breathed against my hand, hurriedly cleaned my teeth.

I went out into the long, deserted corridor. The lighting gave it a mournful, unreal air. I felt unreal too, a figment of my own imagination. Ana's room was at the far end of the corridor. Number 481. I stood outside her door for a long time. Raising my hand to knock. Lowering it. Raising it. I was about to give up, when another door opened nearby. A man came out wearing a dinner suit. I didn't recognise him from the conference. I was making guilty, meaningless, gestures with my still-raised hand. He looked at me with suspicion. He walked towards me. Flight was impossible. I rapped at Ana's door. Nothing. I knocked again, harder.

A sleepy, alarmed voice said, 'Who is it?'

'It's me.'

'Who is it? Hello?'

'It's me.'

The man continued down the corridor, glancing back once or twice.

Ana opened the door, her wavy hair mussed, her eyes questioning. 'Oh. It's you. It's rather late.'

'I know I'm sorry, I—'

'What's wrong? Has something happened?'

'No, I don't think so, I just wanted to...'

She was wearing grey pyjamas with white polka dots. The top had *All you need is love* printed across it. I thought how attractive she looked in the pyjamas: neat, well-proportioned, slight. Without any make-up, she seemed prettier, her features more harmonious, the colouring softer. She tucked a hank of hair behind one ear; my heart raced. She crossed her arms over her chest as if to hide the slogan, deny me a glimpse into her off-duty, private persona.

'What is it?' she said. 'Are you OK?'

'I'm sorry, I couldn't sleep. I was thinking...'

'I've got to get up early, I'm getting the first flight.'

'I know, it's bad timing.' It sounded idiotic.

We stood a couple of feet apart. I was cradling my chin in one hand, as if my head would drop otherwise. The ceiling light directly above me seemed too bright. Ana was smiling, affable but distant.

'I don't know,' I said. 'I was going over our conversation last night, you know, after the conference fiasco.'

'Oh well, that was...'

'I wanted to thank you.'

'You did thank me.'

119

'I mean properly.'

'What, a box of chocolates or something?'

I tried to laugh, but it came out forced. I felt stupid.

I took a deep breath. 'What I mean, Ana, is—'

'I'm not sure what's going on right now. But whatever it is, I don't think I can handle it.'

'No, it's not like that.' I shook my head, rubbed my eye.

'Look,' she said, 'I think it's probably better for all concerned if you to go back to your room.'

'Yeah.'

'Do you want me to walk with you, just to make sure you're all right?' She was still standing in her sentry pose.

'I only wanted to say, I liked so much that you... I mean, what you did.'

'That's OK.' She yawned.

And finally, as I was retreating to the doorway, I managed to spit it out. 'Ana, I wanted to ask you to go, you know, for a meal or something, a date I suppose, erm, not a date exactly, I know it's a strange idea but...'

'Ah. Look. I'm very flattered, and in other circumstances, maybe, you know. Who knows. But no. I mean, we have such a good working relationship.'

'OK, I understand.'

'I'd hate to jeopardise it for something that, erm...'

'You don't mind me asking though?'

'I don't mind.'

She unwrapped her arms, came a step forward and gave me a quick kiss on the cheek. 'Now, go to bed!'

As I walked back to my room I felt proud of myself for having had the nerve, even if only at the final moment, to say something to her and not hide behind mumbled evasions. And at the same time, horribly embarrassed. Forming the thought, then the words to express it, had crystallised my feelings: I wanted her. But I was no nearer to knowing if she was a sexual being at all.

The next morning, as I showered and dressed, I was working on transparent excuses to explain away my behaviour. I would knock on her door, apologise, say I'd had an excruciating migraine, had taken some strong painkillers and what with the alcohol I'd drunk earlier, etcetera. But she wasn't at breakfast and when I asked at reception, she'd already checked out.

***

Over the next few weeks, back in London, I wondered how I might normalise things between us. I thought it would be best to email her in detached, friendly, collegial terms about work: royalties for the edited book, starting some new project, organising a conference. I came up with the idea of a workshop, followed by a new edited volume, on translating puns, anagrams and other forms of wordplay. I drafted a long email, revised it several times to remove all hint of feelings, or any implied reference to events in San Sebastián, and sent it.

She replied the next day, in the same professional tone, expressing enthusiasm for the proposal. She was due to be in London at the end of the month to see academics at UCL and King's, so why didn't we meet up and talk about it? I had a faint flutter of excitement. Could this be a coded way for her to hint that we might talk about *us*?

Three weeks later we were sitting on a café terrace overlooking the river, the same café where I'd last seen Vítor two or three years before.

I got there early, feeling nervous. She arrived bang on time and was her warm, friendly self. It was as if the nocturnal encounter at the San Sebastián hotel had never happened. Yet she conveyed that sense, as she always did, that she was keeping some part of herself in reserve. We discussed the workshop and the edited book, drew up a programme and a high-profile guest list. I did say at one point, 'We'll ask Julia Pinto Hughes of course.'

Ana looked aghast for a moment until she realised I was joking. 'Oh, you're pulling my leg!' She put on a mock-offended face.

I felt a little spark of hope.

We'd finished talking business, but carried on chatting, ordering pastries and more coffee. Ana reminisced about her time at Trinity. How translation studies involved comparing three different English translations of Dante's *Inferno*, alongside the Italian.

'In which circle of hell should Julia Pinto Hughes eventually reside?' I asked.

'I've no idea. You would know better than me.'

'Maybe the circle for those guilty of anger, whichever one that is.'

'The fifth. Yes, that's plausible. Anger.' She considered for a moment. 'Or lust, maybe?'

I couldn't read Ana's expression, but the hopeful part of me wondered whether she might be just a little jealous of Julia, see her as a rival.

'Maybe,' I said.

We began to swap Dante quotes, about whirlwinds and dangerous seas and lamentations. Ana could quote the original Italian, which I more or less understood. It sounded so much better than the English: *Or incomincian le dolenti note a farmisi sentire; or son venuto là dove molto pianto mi percuote.* She fixed her gaze on me as she recited, and I felt the connection between us growing again as if, by accident, I was finding a way through the labyrinth that separated me from her.

My mobile rang. I ignored it until Ana said, 'Please, go ahead. We've more or less finished our business.'

The voice at the other end said, 'Mate! It's been a while.'

It was Mark. I hadn't seen him for a couple of years because he'd been living in Dublin. He said, 'Where are you, cuz?'

'Where you'd expect to find me. In London.'

'In London where?'

I told him.

'Man, I'm just across the river, I'll walk over the

wobbly bridge. Which I'm pleased to say I had no hand in designing.'

'I'm sort of in a meeting, Mark.' Ana was furiously waving her finger like a windscreen wiper to indicate that we weren't. So I said, 'But we're pretty much finished, so yeah, sure, wander over.'

I expected Ana to make her excuses and leave, but she seemed intrigued when I explained to her that Mark had been living in Dublin.

'Doing what?'

'Designing the bridgeworks, I think, for the extension of the DART up to Dublin airport. Something like that. Terribly nerdy.'

'Oh. Interesting. I used to go into university on the DART.'

Ten minutes later Mark was with us. He hugged me and pulled away. He was looking good for someone nearing fifty; in better condition than me at any rate. His face had grown more rugged over the years, while retaining the quizzical charm and the grin.

'Mark, this is Ana Ortega, a colleague from Madrid, she did her Masters at Trinity... Ana, Mark. He's some kind of engineer.'

He kissed her on both cheeks, and said, '*Encantado*,' with not a bad Spanish accent.

Ana smiled. 'Hello Mark. I'm told you're just back from Dublin.'

'Hey,' he said, 'You even have a touch of the Dublin in your accent.' And he was away, pontificating on the differences between Northside rough and Southside posh. Ana was laughing, then she was touching his forearm. Within minutes, he was rolling out some of his evident party pieces: 'Gerrup outeh thahh', and 'Ach, I'm opp te mi bollix in it, so I am.'

'Not bad! For an Englishman.'

'Ah, you couldn't get a fag paper between a Northsider's accent and me own, now.'

123

She arched an eyebrow. 'You could drive a coach and horses through the gap, I'd say.'

I made a stab at bringing the conversation back to topics I felt more comfortable with. 'You've just translated the latest Kevin Barry into Spanish, haven't you, Ana?'

'Not Barry. Brady. That's right. *The Greenway*. It came out in the autumn.' She turned back to Mark.

He said, 'So whereabouts were you living, Ana?'

'Dalkey.'

'Of course.'

'What's that supposed to mean? You were up in the depths of Ballymun no doubt, or Blanchardstown or somewhere.'

I'd never seen her so animated, and the Irish intonation was indeed creeping back into her speech.

'No,' Mark said, 'Ballymun is a bit genteel for the likes of me.'

Ana snorted. 'Ah, you're a divvil, Mark, so you are!'

They laughed.

'Come on,' said Mark, 'we better stop the Irishry, we're excluding your man here.' He put a cousinly arm round me. 'But I could do with eating something.'

'Yes, me too,' said Ana.

I took their order and stood in line at the counter, watching them out of the corner of my eye. At a distance they seemed like raunchy primates, their mutual interest unconcealed. Sourly, I imagined them to be bathed in a fine mist of pheromones.

When I got back to the table with the food, Ana was talking about her translation of the Kevin Brady book. It was a huge autobiographical novel about the financial crash and its aftermath, almost like a gazetteer of Ireland: the hero travels round the country looking for work, doing odd jobs, staying in cheap hostels, eating in awful cafés, drinking away his earnings in unwelcoming pubs, working in the fields alongside Lithuanian migrants.

'So I did some detective work and identified all the

places he mentions,' Ana said, 'and I spent a whole summer travelling round Ireland in an old camper van to track them down. Walked the same streets, drank in the same pubs.'

'Fantastic,' said Mark.

'And then I did my translation.'

'But why?' I asked, irritated by Mark's uncritical admiration. 'What was the point?'

'Well,' Ana said, 'my translation is shortlisted for the Kitchener's Prize, so I guess there was method in my madness.'

'Congratulations!' said Mark, as if he had any clue as to what the Kitchener's was.

'But to answer the question,' she said, looking at me with her professional face, 'I did it to get inside the head of the character, understand what he was going through. Feel what he was feeling. Get a sense of the places. Local colour. Authenticity.'

I realised I didn't know Ana at all, even her professional persona. Realised that it had taken Mark five minutes to establish something new and interesting about her.

When we'd finished eating, Mark said, 'You busy this afternoon?'

'Ana and I have a bit more work to do. Why, what are you—'

'We'd finished our work, hadn't we?' said Ana.

'I was thinking about going to this new museum,' said Mark. 'Sounds pretty wacky. Up in Hackney.'

'What museum?' said Ana.

'Somebody or other's Museum of Curiosities.'

'Hackney? That's a fair old way,' I said.

Ana said, 'We could get a cab.'

'Or take a tube to Bethnal Green,' said Mark.

'I'd love to go,' said Ana.

'Well, if you're both going I guess I'll come along.'

\*\*\*

125

The museum was down a spiral staircase in the underlit basement of a hip burger bar that sold kangaroo and crocodile and ostrich burgers. We descended past trophy animal heads. There was an overpowering smell of sizzling meat. At the bottom was a network of small rooms filled with glass display cases. Ana and Mark hurried ahead of me, gasping and exclaiming, wanting to see it all in one rush, then returning to the beginning to savour everything. I found the basement claustrophobic. And the exhibits were disappointing, a random collection of weird objects trumpeting their own weirdness, striving too hard for effect. It was supposed to be terribly cool and ironic, I guess. I mean, the hairy ballsack of a North American bison, horned blue plastic babies, Siamese-twin skeletons, creepy dolls, giant cockroaches, shrunken heads, animals with grotesque defects preserved in formalin in jars.

And then there were the books. I'd always thought of Ana as serious to the point of dryness, a little too intellectual even for me. But here she was, transformed into a sensual woman, her whole body moving differently as she gawped at eye-wateringly explicit Japanese erotica. She lingered over seamy American volumes from the 1950s, with bright cover illustrations of couples performing what at the time would have been called 'unnatural practices'.

Mark said, 'We always think our generation invented everything in the bedroom, but our old folk must have been at it just like we are.'

I had uncomfortable mental images of my parents and Mark's, and could not reconcile their uptight conventionality with these carefree exhibitionists. I looked at Ana. She was amused, intrigued. Aroused.

Some of the books were not erotica, but jokily displayed alongside them, like schoolboy double entendres. One, in a glass cabinet, was called *Awake My Soul in Joyful Lays*, by the Reverend someone or other.

'That is certainly my aspiration,' said Mark.

Ana frowned, not understanding.

'Joyful lays? Lays? No?'

She caught on and laughed and, something I'd never seen her do, stuck the tip of her tongue out between her teeth.

Next to the joyful lays was a book called *Sex Instruction for Irish Farmers*. The cover had a line drawing of a pair of wellington boots alongside a pair of high-heeled shoes, one of them lying on its side. Mark said, 'Where's the cow?'

'Oh come on!' said Ana in mock reproach.

'What?' Mark put on an innocent face.

'I mean, a sheep, fair enough. But a cow!'

They both giggled. I was, to use an Irishism, gobsmacked. I tried to join in the banter, indicating a book with the imposing title *The History and Social Influence of the Potato. With a Chapter on Industrial Uses.*

'Possibly the sequel to *Sex Instruction for Irish Farmers*,' I said. It sounded lame.

Ana acknowledged the remark with a tilt of her head and a quick smile, but was already turning away to point out to Mark a collection of creepy dolls in a cabinet. One had had its mouth as if surgically removed and reinserted vertically, so it looked like the *vagina dentata* of male nightmare. She said – I'm sure this is what she said – 'You'd need to be careful about how you approached her, eh Mark.'

The remark didn't make much sense if you thought about it, but he was very amused. He said in a cod Irish accent, 'Oh, that you would, now, so you would,' and she laughed yet again.

Feeling like a child shut out of the other kids' game, I began to lag further behind, skulking, cross. When Ana went to the ladies, Mark came up to me.

'She's great.'

'She's a good academic. Excellent translator.'

'You're not... you and her... I mean... Are you?'

'Uh-uh. Not at all. Christ no. We're colleagues.'

'Nice.'

'Mark, look, I've got to go, I've got stuff to do, just say bye to Ana for me.'

'She won't be long I'm sure.'

'No, I'd better be off. Have a good time the pair of you.'

'Cheers! Really great to catch up, let's meet soon, I'll give you a bell.' He turned to look towards the ladies' toilets.

I trudged up the spiral staircase, eased my way through the queuing burger customers and out the door. It was a relief to escape the stifling fug from the griddle. I wondered, with a mixture of admiration and resentment, how on earth Mark had done it, how he'd pierced that neutral, professional carapace that Ana always wore in her dealings with me. I took a deep gulp of the fresh air of the afternoon, surprisingly uplifted – liberated, even – by the belated realisation that she had never been interested in me in the slightest.

# THE HERMENEUTICS OF JULIA PINTO HUGHES

Lisbon in the spring sunshine is a fine place to be, with its smells of coffee, grilled sardines, pungent cheeses, eggy pastries. I'd been once before, in the late 1990s. My most vivid memory, apart from the aromas, was of the Elevador, a free-standing lift in an ironwork tower that carried people up the steep hillside from the Baixa district to the heights of Bairro Alto. Now I was back in the city for a workshop on 'The hermeneutics of literary translation' and I knew I was going to run into Julia Pinto Hughes. It would be the first time since the San Sebastián debacle. But things had been looking up for me since then: a successful talk at a high-level seminar in Toronto, more offers of work, a publisher for my translation of Roberto Tunsch's collected essays on literature.

Julia was giving the keynote address at the opening session of the event in Lisbon, her contribution grandly titled 'Hermeneutics, feminism and the Brazilian novel'. I arrived early on the first morning. Julia was in the lobby, surrounded by acolytes and research students as usual. She noticed me, came over and shook my hand. 'Good to see you,' she said, turning the handshake skilfully into a brief hug, with air kisses.

'Friends, yes?' she said.

'I'm sorry?' Startled by her directness, I retreated behind the shield of my coffee cup.

She smiled. 'Now look, San Sebastián was just the give-and-take, the cut-and-thrust of intellectual debate. I wasn't getting at you. Actually, I thought you handled it all rather well.'

This had to be blatant, insincere ego-soothing, but I felt cheered all the same. Despite the fine weather she wasn't wearing one of her usual sleeveless dresses or sharply tailored skirts, but a long-sleeved white shirt and jeans. She was in good shape. I wondered what she did to keep fit. Whipping students perhaps. Kick-boxing. Something furious and aggressive.

She pulled away, apologetic. 'Have to go and do some deep breathing before my talk. Look, catch up later, OK?' Julia's address was more interesting than I'd expected. She had a real passion for the writings of Alma Sertão and the other *grandes dames* of Brazilian letters. She knew exactly what she was doing, having somehow gained huge intellectual assurance since the Lima days. By sheer force of will she'd turned into a competent academic. Or maybe I'd arrogantly got her wrong, underestimated her, all along.

The academic audience applauded her talk with enthusiasm. She was a star in her own production, relishing the spotlight: scarcely the discreet, invisible translator of tradition. If you want to be *visible*, I thought, shouldn't you just be a conference interpreter? But then conference interpreters were audible rather than visible, given they were magicked away behind smoked glass in insulated booths. Which made me think of Sonja, and of us failing to have sex in a booth, back in the heyday of our relationship in Paris.

Though the talk was polished, I wasn't convinced by the arguments and wanted to probe her further. I also had the childish urge to point out to the rapt hall that 'hermeneutics' comes from the Greek for 'to interpret' or 'translate', so the 'hermeneutics of translation' is a tautology. But the chair did her best not to see my raised hand.

At the end of the session, I waited for Julia to pull herself away from the throng of over-excited doctoral students.

'Interesting, thought-provoking,' I said.

'Thanks, glad you liked it.'

'Though I still have quite a few questions about what you said.'

She looked at her watch. 'Tonight they're taking me out to dinner, but why don't we go and grab a coffee now, if you've time? Carry on with the discussion. I'd be interested in your views.' She saw my hesitation. Turning her head to indicate the gaggle of students, she said, 'Come on, save me from the groupies.'

We took a tram in the direction of the Tagus, got off near the Praça dom Pedro, with its wavy black and white stone pattern, like some Viennese glazed pastry. We left the square and walked through the cobbled streets. Julia seemed to know where she was going. Up a steep side street, we came to one of Lisbon's old coffee shops. Inside, the décor was sober: sepia woodwork, cream walls, a grey flagstone floor, a handful of old black and white photographs of serious, intellectual-looking men in hats, possibly writers. The only concession to frivolity was the coffee grinder with its the bright red and brass fittings.

'This is where you get the best espressos outside Italy,' Julia said. She inhaled the aromas in a way that was almost sensual. 'In the old days, when my family lived here, you'd order your own blend from the local coffee shop and they'd keep a note of it in a book, and mix it for you to be collected.'

'So you lived here?'

I vaguely remembered she had a Portuguese connection.

'Yes, my paternal grandfather was Portuguese, hence the "Pinto". Though my dad was born in England. We lived here for four years from when I was ten. Quite a turbulent period after the Salazar dictatorship, democracy coming back and all that, I remember that soldier guy with a monocle, what was his name?' She stared ahead trying to remember for a couple of seconds before continuing. 'Spinola, that was it. Anyway, my father was head of the English school here. Then we went back home. I always used to make fun of him for his terrible Portuguese accent. I was a bit embarrassed by him.'

'So you learned your Portuguese here?'

'Yes.'

That answered the puzzle as to why her Portuguese

accent sounded (to my ears) natural, whereas her Spanish accent didn't.

'We have something in common. I lived in The Hague as a kid, and learned Dutch.'

'I think I knew you spoke Dutch,' she said. I must have mentioned it to her on some occasion in the distant past. I was flattered she'd remembered.

We sat at a marble-topped table and the waiter brought our drinks. I sipped my espresso; it tasted strong and earthy. Julia downed hers in one and called over the waiter to order another, together with a plate of *pastels de nata*, Portuguese custard tarts.

'So,' I said, 'as you tell it, translation is a political, radically democratic act in a naughty world.'

She laughed. 'I do think that issues of power and gender politics underlie any cultural product, and that the job of the translator is to reinterpret these in a way that challenges power structures.' She went on about hierarchies of causation, about hermeneutical versus essentialist approaches, about gender relations.

I said, 'Is that why it's called *her*meneutics?'

'What? Oh! Ha-ha.' She reflected for moment. '*His*meneutics could be a phallocentric interpretation of the world.'

'Like *his*tory and *her*story?'

'Exactly.'

'But isn't the danger that you just slip into relativist bullshit? That anything goes, that the text is whatever you want it to be?'

Julia took a bite of the *pastel*, holding it delicately in her fingers, and, unembarrassed, stuck out her tongue to lick a crumb from below her bottom lip. 'Mmm,' she said, 'have some,' and she held up the mutilated tart for me to take a bite. I lunged for it with open mouth and a bit broke off and fell into my coffee.

'Oops,' she said.

I fished out the soggy lump with my teaspoon. 'Surely,'

I persisted, 'the reader doesn't want a radical-feminist interpretation of Alma Sertão, she or he wants to know what Alma Sertão actually wrote. As close as possible given all the uncertainties.'

Julia echoed my words back to me. '"*What Alma Sertão actually wrote.*" And what did she actually write?' She leaned back in her chair and put one arm behind her head in a challenging posture. The move emphasised the form of her breast under her shirt. My eye was drawn involuntarily to the tanned, swelling 'V' of flesh against the white of the fabric where the top two buttons were open. She caught my eye and I felt myself blush. She did not seem offended or put out, but had the hint of a smile, as if amused by her power over me in that moment.

I stammered, 'I mean, the words on the page. It's out there in black and white, isn't it. We have to assume that what she wrote is what she intended to say.'

Julia leaned forward again. 'Who's to judge what she intended? What if she changed her mind? People find new interpretations that the author wasn't aware of. And when broader power relations change, the range of possible interpretations widens.'

'Hmm...'

'And we translators should be active agents in that.'

'Really?'

'Yes. There's some radical reappraisal going on. I even heard someone say in a public lecture recently that translators who think there's some essential original text to discover should be taken out and shot. Now I'm not saying I agree with them, but...' She was looking at me slyly, waiting for my reaction.

'Bit harsh.'

I wondered fleetingly if a man who glanced at a woman's cleavage – even without meaning to, perhaps out of shyness or a fear of meeting her eyes – should also be taken out and shot.

I said, 'I have this old-fashioned belief that the

translator's job is to be faithful to the original.'

'People go on about translation loss. Why are people always going on about loss as if they're mourning something, when they should be celebrating a new perspective, an imaginative rereading? They want fidelity to the original, for Christ's sake, but there's no such thing.'

Julia finished off another custard tart and licked her fingers. She leaned forward and stared at me, eyes narrowing. 'Fidelity is so overrated, don't you think?'

I thought, *Jesus Christ, Julia's coming on to me.*

'Actually,' she continued, 'the original doesn't constrain the translator that much. You can privilege or downplay certain aspects. Some people start with the sound of the story, the music of it, for instance. The melody, the rhythm...'

I had a flash of memory, of dancing with Julia in Lima to Lionel Richie's 'All Night Long', of her breath on my ear. I felt intense nostalgia for the distant moment.

'And that's how you worked on Alma Sertão?'

'Absolutely. Hear the song she's singing, if you like.'

Julia shuffled her feet under the table, and I felt the faintest brush of the fabric of her jeans against my trousers.

'OK. I get it. Interpretation is a big part of what translators do. They're always making decisions about style, meaning, the sound and rhythms of the original. So why make such a theoretical song-and-dance about it, why give fancy names to something we do anyway?'

I felt invigorated, aroused, by this intellectual give-and-take, the sense of crossing swords with a tough opponent who'd fight back. I stretched my legs, hoping to come up against Julia's calf, but there was no contact.

'Yes, you're right, it's what we do anyway. But only intuitively. The point is to make it systematic, change the way people think about the act of translation.' She licked her finger and used it to pick up the stray crumbs of custard tart from the plate. 'Also it's about how to educate the new generation of translators.'

'I don't do much teaching, I'm just a jobbing translator, not an academic.'

'Of course you are.'

'And if you only knew how and what I teach, you'd say I was poisoning impressionable young minds.' She leaned across the table and put her head close to mine, mock-interrogator style. 'And *are* you?'

We grinned at each other. She put her hand on my wrist. 'Hey, you remember how they used to teach us at the Institute? Be faithful to the source text, minimise translation loss. They encouraged us to be a sort of text impersonator.' She put on a gushing voice: '"Oh, you *do* do a good Benedetti, it sounds just like him!"'

I laughed. I wasn't sure if she was having a dig at my translation of Benedetti's story, 'The Night of the Ugly'.

'But also,' she continued, 'you were told to aim for "readability". The ideal review was one that said, "It doesn't read like a translation"!'

'Quite.'

'It's contradictory, isn't it? Be identical to the original, but also be perfectly accessible to the English reader. Huh? Why did we even put up with it?'

'Interesting times,' I said. 'We were the impressionable young minds back then.'

I was disappointed she'd withdrawn her hand from my arm.

'Oh yes. Some good times. And some unfinished business.' She was looking at me directly. 'What with earthquakes and whatnot.'

I lowered my eyes, examined the inside of my coffee cup, twiddled the teaspoon, clinked it down on the saucer. I was caught between excitement at the spark between us, and fear of taking it too far.

'But you landed on your feet after you left Lima.'

'Yes,' she said. 'I came to Portugal, did my Masters at Coimbra. It all worked out in the end.'

'It certainly did.'

135

'For you too,' she said.

'I'm not sure about that.'

She narrowed her eyes, as if in annoyance at my self-deprecating shtick. 'Still fishing for compliments?'

I frowned, pretending not to understand what she meant. She smiled at my dissembling, in control. I glanced at my phone.

'Look, Julia, I should be getting back to my hotel.'

'You have plans?'

'No, not really, it's just—'

'We're going in the same direction, I'll walk with you.'

She paid the bill without fuss, and wouldn't let me contribute. 'I ate all the tarts,' she said.

We left the café and ambled, talking about the conference, work. Nothing too intimate. There were graffiti everywhere, on the walls of buildings, over the yellow and white trams. Down a cobbled side street, I caught a glimpse of the Elevador de Santa Justa.

'Look,' I said, pointing. 'It's about the only thing I remember from when I was here fifteen years ago. That and the custard tarts.'

She laughed. 'Have you ever been up? All the way to the top?'

'No.'

'Come on then.' She took my arm and we wheeled round and walked together towards the Elevador with its intricate ironwork and strange flat hat of a viewing platform. We rose, clanking, with the smells of old cable grease and the sea breeze. At the top, we leaned on the railing and looked out over the estuary of the Tagus and, to the west, the ocean. Julia was close enough for me to feel the touch of her arm through my shirt, and smell that perfume of hers, woody and refined. This was a new Julia. Or perhaps not. Perhaps she had always been open to multiple interpretations, and my reading of her had been too narrow.

She took a vape out of her handbag and sucked on it;

she must have given up the cigarettes. After a few puffs, she turned to face me.

'How did the edited volume go down, in the end?'

She'd caught me off-guard again. I'd been hoping we could both genteelly pretend that the falling-out in Madrid hadn't happened.

I took a breath. 'What, the thing on translation in Europe... the thing I edited, erm, that Ana Ortega and I edited?'

'Yes, that thing. With her. The thing that didn't have my chapter in it because you thought it was crap.'

'It's not that we—'

'Don't look so worried. Water under the bridge, *águas passadas*.' She rubbed my arm. 'In all honesty, not my best effort, I had too many things on, too many deadlines, too many idiots demanding stuff. It's just...'

'Just what?'

'Nothing. You, I could deal with, we'd probably have come to some kind of understanding. But I couldn't be doing with Ana Ortega.'

'Ana?'

'Yes, Ana. With her prim little *mosquita muerta* face. Jesus. And you blokes fall for it. Though I'm sure she's very good at what she does.'

I was going to protest, but I thought of Ana and Mark in the Museum of Curiosities and stayed silent.

Julia said brightly, 'Anyway. Enough of that.' She put her arm through mine and turned with me back towards the railings. 'Just look at this fucking amazing view.'

The rest of the afternoon had a choreographed inevitability to it. We got to the hotel, sat at the bar and sampled the ports. My calves ached from the steep cobbled streets. It seemed natural to have a late lunch together in a little restaurant down a quiet alley, more wine. We became touchy-feely with each other and laughed as we devised ever more baroque and fiendish punishments for essentialists and hermeneuticists alike.

The conversation turned back to Peru, our reminiscences of Lima, her mystifying hatred of Peruvian food. I asked about her fling with my flatmate Javier, and she made me laugh treacherously at her graphic account of his bedroom etiquette. There was an awkward pause as we took in the fact that we'd never got to experience each other's bedroom etiquette.

She said, 'In those days I thought you were a bit intimidating, actually.'

'What?'

'Yes. Intellectually intimidating, arrogant. Had it all worked out.'

'If only. And funny how things change. I mean, you're so well known these days.'

'I remember that way you had of sitting on the edge of things at parties. Staring into space, a bit aloof.'

'That was actual shyness.'

'Oh, come off it, there's no such thing, shyness is just an excuse.'

I thought about arguing but I realised that it was flattering she remembered all this, and that it was Julia's version of me, her interpretation, her reading of what I amounted to.

'Anyway,' she said, 'it worked on me.'

I didn't respond, I couldn't quite believe I'd heard her right. And if I had, what exactly had she meant by the remark? I started to talk about Peruvian food, and the police riot when we were there, and our trip to the wine district with Gabi and the others. And, inevitably, and in the manner of Basil Fawlty, I couldn't stop myself from mentioning the earthquake.

'So eerie,' I said. 'You think the world is stable, and suddenly it really isn't.'

'Terrifying is the word I'd use.'

'The earthquake, that was why you left, wasn't it?'

'What? No. Where did you get that idea from?'

'From those Americans you shared a flat with. They

told me—'

'No. That's not correct. I left because I got a message to say my father was seriously ill and I should get the first flight to England.'

'Oh, I'm sorry.'

'No, it was such a long time ago.'

'But you never did come back to Lima.'

'No, because my mum was stressed out with my dad's illness, and I wanted to be closer to home in case something happened.'

I thought I'd put a dampener on our mood, but Julia shrugged and raised her glass. 'To Peru!' she said. 'To what might have been.' We clinked glasses.

After a digestif or two, we stumbled out, arms linked, laughing at ourselves and the situation, and ended up snogging in the little back street, like teenagers. I felt transgressive, a middle-aged man caught up in a delicious hormonal rush with a middle-aged woman.

We went up in the lift to her hotel room. When she took off her shirt, there were patches of thickened dry skin, flaking and reddish in places, on the backs of her arms, and one or two coin-sized plaques on her stomach. She gave a defenceless, apologetic twitch of her mouth.

'You OK?' I asked.

'You know, it's a skin thing. Psoriasis.' She sat down on the bed. I sat beside her.

'I had it badly as a kid. All over my body. On my face, my scalp. Had to use all kinds of ointments and bandages. Some with tar in, so I stank. The kids at school called me pooey Pinto.'

'It's not too bad.' I put my arm round her. Her eyes, up close, were not so dark and gimlet-sharp, they had little marks of colour in them, muddy greens and ambers.

'When I was an adolescent,' she said, 'it started to go, and by my twenties it had gone completely.'

I gave her a chaste kiss on the shoulder.

'Then last year it started coming back. They say it

comes and goes in cycles. There are better drugs these days, but they've got side effects. So. I'm a self-conscious teenager again.'

Hard, determined, vengeful Julia. I hugged her. She let herself be hugged. I'd fixated on that hardness, the self-serving implacability. Had failed to see the vulnerability.

She turned to me at the same moment as I turned to her, and we kissed. There was something in it that was almost tenderness, or closeness, more than simple lust. Then we were lying on the bed, helping each other out of our clothes, awkward at first, then slowing and relaxing, hardly speaking. She turned away to place a packet of condoms on the bedside table beside the vape.

If I'd ever thought or fantasised about it, I would have imagined Julia to be energetic and overbearing in bed. But she lay sleek and waiting for my touch, wanting to be pampered. *Stroke me*, her body seemed to say (*on my terms only, mind*). She stretched back on the sheets. 'Kiss me,' she murmured. Eyes closed. A half-smile. And she arched her back, slowly, like a slow stretching yawn. Later, she took over, and for once I didn't feel guilty just lying there, feeling pleasure.

We finished, and almost at once she rolled away and reached for her vape. She lay against the headboard and took a drag. It smelled spicy, perfumed. Cloves and cardamom maybe. She seemed to relax deeply.

'So,' she said, with a mischievous glint, 'did the earth move for you?'

We both laughed: something else I'd discounted in her was a sense of humour.

I dozed off.

Later, someone was shaking me and I awoke. Julia was looking down at me. She was fully dressed.

'Chop, chop,' she said. 'I have to get ready for my dinner, so…'

'Christ, did I fall asleep?'

I eased myself from the bed, conscious of her eyes

on me, and searched for my discarded underpants. I was feeling the beginnings of a hangover. While I got dressed, she stood leaning her bottom against the writing desk, arms folded.

As I was tying my shoelaces, I said, 'Could we maybe meet up again later, I mean after your dinner engagement?'

'I don't think that's going to work for me.'

'But we seem to have had a good time together, couldn't we—?'

'Hey, whoa!' she said.

I was alarmed at the edge to her voice. 'Apologies, I just thought, maybe we could—'

'Uh-uh.' It was that sound mothers make to tell children not to eat food off the floor.

Seeing my stricken face she added, more emollient. 'OK, sorry. I just want to be clear. It's been fun. You know what they say, pleasure deferred is all the sweeter. Or something.' Again, the mischievous grin. 'But, as far as I'm concerned, that's it.'

It was like a world shifting rapidly under my feet, once and then again. Instead of shutting up and departing with my dignity intact, I found myself arguing it out with her.

'But Julia, we've waited two decades to actually talk to each other. To have some kind of exchange that wasn't academic and/or hostile. I thought that... I thought there seemed to be, I don't know, a rapport. A connection. Can't we at least explore...?' I ground to a halt.

She thrust a hank of hair brutally behind her ear. 'Look, I'm in a relationship.'

'Oh, Christ! I'm sorry.'

'What are you apologising for? It's not like you've led me astray.' She smiled at the idea. I thought of her comment in the café about fidelity being overrated.

'I'm with a guy who's divorced, like me,' she said. 'Not wanting to be tied down. So we've got our own houses. Space to breathe. But in a funny way, we're committed.'

I sighed.

'The last thing I want is another man moping around over me.'

I said, 'I'm not the moping type.' This was probably a lie.

She rubbed my forearm. 'Good.'

I added, 'Can't we just leave it open-ended?'

She looked for her vape, and took a puff. It was as if she was trying to defuse the tension in the question, lighten it. 'Well I suppose our paths are bound cross from time to time. Workshops. Conference season. We could easily coincide and, who knows, if the conditions are right…'

'If the stars align?'

'Something like that.'

'Enemies with benefits?' That sounded less amusing than I'd intended, more wounded.

'I never saw us as enemies. Sometimes as competitors.'

'Competitors with benefits?'

'OK. But don't get your hopes up.'

She smiled and stroked my shoulder, gave me a quick kiss on the lips. Gently but firmly she guided me to the door. I walked back down the hotel stairs to my room, with the faint scent in my nostrils of custard, cardamom, sex.

Not so long after the Lisbon encounter with Julia, I was in Leiden again, to research in the archives of the university and the Hortus Botanicus. It was my first visit there since the break-up with Rachel nearly a decade earlier, and the familiar streets around the Morspoort where we'd stayed, and between there and the botanical gardens, seemed to retain the emotional aftertaste of our difficult moments. Still, it's a beautiful town, and *gezellig* as the Dutch would say – comfortable, cosy, welcoming. I'd done an intensive Dutch refresher course there one summer in the late 1980s, and it didn't take long for older, happier memories to resurface as I strolled the narrow streets along the canals, with their pleasing jumble of architectural styles. It was soothing for my nerves, jarred by the frantic bustle of London.

A university contact suggested that my visit would be a good opportunity for me to do a reading from my translation of *Malign Fragments*. I agreed, and it went quite well, with an audience mainly of attentive Masters students from the Language Centre. And possibly because my own teeth were in one of their periodic flare-ups, I chose to read a passage recounting the moment when Roberto Tunsch's repulsive, foul-breathed hero, Adolfo Tarir Espósito, visits the dentist to have his mouth examined. It included the following:

> The dentist, who had strapped to his broad and curving forehead a giant squid's eye of an amplifying mirror, peered into Adolfo's stretched mouth before inserting a kind of miniature snub-nosed forceps. Over the clinic's sound system, Adolfo would later recall, The Beatles' 'Here, There and Everywhere' was playing, with its lusciously facile melody. Adolfo was expecting a lengthy examination, an uncomfortable probing

towards the back of his throat, a triggering of his gag reflex. But in seconds the dentist had withdrawn his hand and, with an agile flick of the wrist, he presented before Adolfo's eyes a small whitish-greyish object. It was about the size of a blood-swollen sheep tick, or perhaps a kernel of sweetcorn.

The dentist said, 'It was attached to the side of the uvula, rather posterior, so requiring a somewhat flexible instrument. This is the source of the issue, I'm convinced of it.'

'What? This?' Adolfo said, offended almost by the insignificance of the object.

'Ah,' said the dentist, 'do not underestimate the power of the intensely inspissated adhesion, nurtured over months or even years with layers of slowly compacting organic matter. You will find here a concentration of sulphides and mercaptans of which a research chemist or an enraged skunk would be proud.'

'Excellent.' Here was the holy grail of halitosis, the inspissated adhesion. 'Put it in some container for me. I'll keep it as a memento.'

The dentist held it to his nose and swished it around as if a glass of fine wine. 'The odours are volatilising nicely,' he said, 'but will only be fully released on breaking the slightly crusted surface of the adhesion.'

As Adolfo walked through the softly exhaling automatic doors of the clinic, he considered three things: first, the intense sensory experience that awaited him when he finally crushed the grain between his thumb and finger, releasing its heady power. Second, that perhaps, deprived of this glowing particle of organic plutonium, he'd lose his strength, his powers over others, be like Samson shorn, Superman at the mercy of Kryptonite. And third, that he would never be able to listen in the same way again to 'Here, There and Everywhere', for it would be impregnated, chronically, inexpungibly, with the savour and atmosphere of this experience, with its penetrating odour.

As I walked along the Rapenburg in the rain after the talk, I felt the pulsing in my jaw, and a deep burrowing nervy pain. It subsided, but I was tensed up waiting for it to recur. When it came again, it was stronger still. Another dying nerve root, I thought. I got back to my accommodation and phoned an acquaintance to get the name of a good local dentist.

The following day, Cornelius van de Varen examined me with care, felt the biting surfaces, wiggled the teeth, looked at them under magnification. He told me that my nerve roots were fine, that my pain was probably due to anxiety, and that I had a tendency to clench my jaw.

'You are a bruxist,' he said. It sounded like a moral failing.

'I'm sorry?'

'It is the same in English. *Bruxism.*' He saw my puzzled look. 'You grind your teeth.'

'Ah.'

'It weakens and loosens them, damages your jaw, disturbs your sleep. Are you a particularly nervous person?'

I worked my jaw from side to side to relieve the stiffness.

'I'd advise an occlusal splint,' he said. 'A special tooth guard.'

'I see.'

'I'll take a cast, and we'll have it through in a week.'

I nodded. How often did Adolfo Tarir Espósito go to the dentist, I wondered, and did the latter have to wear a super-strength latex facemask to avoid fainting from the sulphurous fumes?

'Do you do treatments for halitosis?' I asked, alarmed that my thoughts had broken through into the outer world.

'Certainly,' said van de Varen. 'Though your oral hygiene is good. Much of the time halitosis is simply the unvarnished evidence of our condition as animals – eaters of meat and of other organic matter that decays. Halitosis is life, you might say.'

'An interesting way of looking at it.'

'You can pick up a brochure on all our tariffs at the reception desk.'

I left the dental surgery and followed the gentle curve of the Rapenburg in the direction of the station. It started to rain again, and outside a pizzeria I stopped to look at the menu. A waitress appeared and asked me in English if I needed any help. I replied in Dutch, asking what the day's 'special' was, and what time they stopped serving. She looked at me blankly. 'Sorry, do you speak English?' she said. She stood there, hip cocked, one hand on her waist, short, dark and pretty. 'Yes,' I replied, 'but you don't speak Dutch?' 'No,' she said, 'I'm from Andorra.' She smiled and shrugged.

I thanked her and left, preferring the rain. I walked back towards Apothekersdijk, and for a moment I wondered if there was any point to it at all, if everyone spoke the lingua franca and nobody bothered to learn other languages. I reproved myself for being sniffy about other people's lack of linguistic skills: translating books for such people was my bread and butter, after all. I'd built a reasonably successful career out of it. As if to make amends, at least inwardly, I turned about and walked back to the restaurant. The pretty waitress smiled at me as I went in and sat down. Seeing her made me realise why I'd returned: her looks and posture reminded me of someone. Gabi. The fellow student on the literary translation course in Lima, back in the 1980s, with whom I'd been ridiculously infatuated.

Of course, I'd not seen her for nearly a quarter of a century, but I'd often fantasised about meeting up with her again. The unconsummated affair nagged at me for years, because I felt I'd missed my moment, *the* moment, and that such opportunities didn't recur. My rational mind assured me that it was nonsense, that if it wasn't *this* one, it would be *that* one. But something about Gabi insinuated

146

to me that this possibility was unique. It was true that I'd never found anyone to replace her, there was no one I felt anything like as passionate about. At least not for longer than a month or two.

Probably it wouldn't have worked out with Gabi either. After I came back to Europe, I drifted from relationship to relationship. It became a pattern, a habit. Four years was my record, with Rachel. And that was in two stretches, the second like a suspended prison term invoked for misbehaviour. Among the relationships were the occasional affairs or flings, making no pretence to be other than transient.

Such thoughts turned me a little morose. In my younger, more masochistic days, I would say to myself that I drifted in the current, that I was a second-rater. That was the inspissated kernel of unsavoury truth to be extracted from the layers of my history. I'd roll it between my fingers until it released its stench, which I'd breathe in with a mixture of fascination and self-disgust. As I grew older, my responses became less melodramatic, more indulgent towards my own failings. Though I did still sometimes wonder if I could have done more in life, done better. But doesn't everybody? Now, sitting in the pizzeria finishing off the stodgy remains of my *Quattro stagioni*, I told myself to get a grip, forget all the might-have-beens, and go back to work.

\*\*\*

A week or two later, I did an afternoon's work at the university library. I came out into the early evening throng and jostle of foreign students, sent to Leiden for their semester abroad or to do intensive courses in the Dutch language. To escape those over-loud American and English voices, I crossed the Rapenburg and sauntered east towards the Nieuwe Rijn. Up a narrow side street I saw the entrance to the Burcht, the old city fortification

147

built to protect inhabitants from the frequent floods. The top of the Burcht is the highest point in Leiden, a place to survey the whole panorama of the city. Yet despite that, when you are in the network of narrow streets nearby you could be unaware of the Burcht's existence: it is more or less invisible behind buildings. So you always come upon it suddenly, and almost by surprise, even when you know it's there.

Now on this bright evening I walked through the entrance gate with its crested stone columns and climbed the paths winding up the grassy mound of the old motte. As usual at this time of day, it was almost deserted.

I leant against the circular rampart walls looking west at the blazing, thunderous sky over the Vermeer-red tiles of the rooftops and the domes of the churches. I kept feeling my jaw, hardly believing it was any less seized-up and painful, convinced that van de Varen's expensive tooth guard was a waste of money.

I was opening my jaws to their full extent and slowly closing them to test their stiffness when a voice close behind me murmured, 'You again!'

I turned, startled and feeling like an idiot with my mouth half open. 'Christ!' I said. 'What are *you* doing here?'

It was Sonja Arendshof. Apart from a very brief and rather frosty exchange at a conference in Seville a few years before, I hadn't seen her since we were going out together in Paris, back in the 1990s. Then, I'd briefly wondered whether she might be the new Gabi, but I succeeded in misreading things to the point where I scuppered our relationship, and it couldn't be salvaged. These things seem so obvious looking back, but in the moment I'd been convinced I was acting reasonably at every step.

'Look at you!' Sonja said, taking hold of my arm.

What did she mean? Was it a reference to my changed appearance, all the banal and unavoidable signs of ageing – the incipient double chin, the still-clenched jaw, the hairline receding from the temples? The slouch. The small but undeniable paunch. I could blame Rachel for this last one: she had liked to feed me up, as if preparing me for the slaughter, and I'd never bothered to lose the pounds gained. These days no doubt she would have said I had a 'dad bod'. And would have added resentfully, 'Without even being a dad!' Perhaps she believed that the extra flesh she put on me made me more hers, less likely to become someone else's.

On top of the Burcht, under Sonja's critical gaze, it flashed through my mind that it was time I considered a regime of physical training. Yoga, perhaps, or tennis. Nothing too strenuous.

I said, 'I know, I know. I should do more exercise.' As I said it, I wondered if Sonja hadn't simply meant, *here's looking at you,* celebrating the fact that her eyes were on the face of an old friend, an old lover.

She stretched out an arm, rubbed my shoulder, smiled. 'Good to see you, *vieze Engelsman.*' Gone was the coolness of our previous brief encounter in Seville. 'You're not too bad. For an old guy.'

She was only a couple of years younger than me, but in much better shape.

'You're looking great,' I said.

'Hm,' she said.

'Hm,' I replied.

'You like it here?'

'It's beautiful, isn't it.'

She was staring over the city. I followed her gaze to the church domes and spires, the couples in courtyards below us, an old woman on a balcony shooing seagulls away. A gull mewed close.

'It's an artificial museum of a place. Not real.' She turned to me with a faint smile. 'Is that why you like it? Because it's not real life?'

When we'd been together, I'd have risen to the bait, replied in kind. But that's one advantage of age: your reflexes slow, you have more time to think before you speak. So I reined myself in.

'And you?' I said. 'How are you doing?'

'Me? Good, I guess. Things are different.' She took a deep breath. 'I have a seven-year-old son now. Lucas.'

'You have a seven-year-old son? Wow, you didn't have a son when I last saw you. Has it been that long? Anyway, congratulations. A son.'

'Uh-huh.'

'And a husband, I imagine?'

She shook her head. 'No current husband.'

'So, on your own?'

'No, I have a son.'

'I meant—'

'I know what you meant. Yes, on my own. And you?'

'Yes. Currently.'

'*Currently*,' she repeated. 'Hm. Currently.'

We were silent for a while, both of us leaning against the brick ramparts, looking at the horizon.

'Do you still work the international conference circuit?'

'Yeah,' she said. 'Still. Less, though. Because of Lucas.' She grinned at me. 'Or do you mean do I still fool around with all the good-looking Swedish interpreters in the conference hotels?'

It had been twenty years ago that I'd made the implied accusation, during the row that would prove terminal. 'I never said you... Look, you left me, not the other way round!' I meant to sound annoyed in a light-hearted, even jokey, way, but I didn't bring it off; she'd scratched a scabbed-over wound.

'Yes,' Sonja said, 'you were a total *klootzak*.'

'True, I suppose.'

'Such a *klootzak*. I always thought your translations were your friends. Your lovers too, maybe.'

My imaginary friends. She had a point; Rachel often said similar things about me and my translations.

'Ouch,' I said. 'That's harsh.'

150

'But you had your good points.' Her tone was caressing and teasing again.

'Did I?'

'Uh-huh.'

We had turned to face each other, the Burcht and Leiden and my stiff jaw blocked from consciousness. And then – maybe, I don't know, because we were alone on top of the Burcht, in the unreal glow of the late evening light, lulled by the gentle rustle of the leaves – we were talking together in our joshing way, but without the caustic undertow, the hurt and hurtful subtext. It was like in the old Paris days: intimate, jokey, tactile. I felt a long-unfamiliar emotion, a sort of skipping of the heart.

The sun had gone below the horizon and it was getting cold. 'Shall we go and have a drink?' I said. 'Or do you have to get back for your son?'

'No, as it happens. I've left him with his little friend in Wassenaar for couple of nights while I'm in Leiden. I'm visiting an old aunt of mine, there wouldn't be anything in it for Lucas, she's very deaf, the old dear.'

\*\*\*

We found a little café, sat with beers and a plate of cold meat and cheeses, and we caught up, switching casually back and forth between English and Dutch. After a while, we talked more about the break-up.

'I don't think you ever realised what it was like for me,' Sonja said, 'the conference interpreting. You were convinced that literary translation was the hardest job ever.'

'I don't think I ever thought—'

'*So many decisions, so many difficult choices!* Whether to keep the strangeness, the foreignness of the text or to make it read smoothly in English, how to translate all those puns and plays on words, how to render regional dialects, etcetera, etcetera. You see, I was paying attention.

But Jesus, you didn't half bang on about it! As if it was a matter of life and death.'

'I did not. Did I?'

'Yes. And I guess for you it really was life and death. Your life, your way of operating in the world. But you never seemed to wonder what my life was like.'

'So what was it like? Tell me.'

'Now you ask!'

She shook her head, as if at the enormity of the task of explaining. 'You have no idea unless you've done it, what it's like to be a conference interpreter. You have to reset your brain to juggle the two languages. Listen in one, speak in the other. *At the same time.*' She gripped my wrist. 'Try it! I bet you never have.'

'Not really, no.'

'Imagine, you're interpreting the speech of some bigwig or other. Sometimes they make it up as they go along so you don't even have notes. Or it's a specialist area, like a convention on underwear. Would you know the Spanish for sports bra, slip, tanga, boxer shorts? The other interpreters used to laugh at me because I'd shut my eyes to concentrate, and I'd wave my hands about like crazy. Once I did a fetishists' convention... I didn't even understand the Dutch or English words, let alone the Russian! So you make lists of the key words and pray you can find the right one quickly enough.'

She stopped to take a long draught of beer.

'And then when people start asking stupid questions of the speaker – do you translate what they actually say, or what you think they might mean?' She looked at me. 'You know, it's intense, your brain hurts. Half hour on, half hour off. For eight hours. Jesus!'

She was speaking with urgency, as if talking about it had put her back there, in the interpreters' booth.

'I used to come home, wrung out. Sometimes you'd drop round to see me and you just didn't get it. I'd still be wired, adrenaline surge, you rabbiting on about some

152

Peruvian novel, or your office politics or something. I couldn't sit, couldn't eat, couldn't read. I certainly couldn't listen to you. Jesus. I'd be so wound up, so aroused. I don't mean sexually. Or do I? Maybe I do? Maybe I should have just jumped you!' She laughed, and reached across and chucked me under the chin. 'But you were always so… So English.'

'Me!'

'Yes! Like setting time slots for sex.'

At the next table was a silent couple, younger than us. The man peered round at Sonja when he heard the word *sex*.

'I did not set time slots.'

'Yes. It was like the school curriculum. Saturday mornings. Wednesday evenings after two glasses of wine.'

'Come on, that's an exaggeration.'

'Yeah, maybe. A bit. Not too much. Where were the drunken fumblings, the hot, sweaty middle-of-the-night ones? Or outside, even?'

I had the sense of yet again having misread, misjudged, been obtuse. I sighed. 'I did sometimes wonder why you were with me.'

'Me too,' said Sonja. 'Idiot! Enough of the self-pity, for Christ's sake. I was with you because I *liked* you. You made me laugh – when you weren't being all serious and self-important about translation. And, frankly, because you could make me, you know…'

'Make you what?'

'You know. It was a knack and you managed it. Probably by accident. I had much handsomer boyfriends than you, with—'

'Great. Thanks.'

'But they didn't necessarily, you know, manage it. You had the knack. So.'

She'd said '*het trucje*': the little trick. The words stuck in my mind like an earworm. The man at the next table was trying to pretend he wasn't listening to our conversation.

153

His partner stared straight ahead of her, disapproving of him, disapproving of us.

Sonja had noticed the couple too. She said in a louder voice, 'And of course the anal sex was fantastic. And the bondage.'

The man coloured and looked away, anywhere but at his partner. Sonja wiggled her eyebrows at me, and I giggled, a *fou rire* that made me turn to the wall and cover my face with my hands.

'Hmm,' said Sonja, 'maybe we should talk dirty more often.'

'Yes. Maybe.'

Before long the man's head was twisting our way again. The woman glowered at him, furious. That set me off again. To regain control I had to bite the inside of my mouth hard enough to make it bleed.

She sighed. 'Lots of maybes.'

'Yep.'

'Maybe you shouldn't have been such a bastard.'

'Maybe.'

'Oh, but it wasn't really about you and that American bitch. Basically it was that you never made the effort to see what things were like for me. I mean, my work, my daily life.'

'Yeah, I'm sorry, I should have—'

'I don't know. So wrapped up in your own stuff.' She shook her head, smiled, compressed her lips. 'But I guess I was wrapped up in my stuff too. Maybe I... I don't know.'

As we left the café, Sonja threaded her arm through mine, a gesture that seemed surprising yet so familiar. It felt natural that we should go home together. I suggested she come back to my rented attic room off the Lange Mare. But she wanted to go to her aunt's. 'Don't worry,' she said, 'she's deaf, my bedroom is on the ground floor. The staircase is very steep, and she's got arthritis so she doesn't come downstairs unless she has to. We'll be fine.'

The house was in a narrow *steeg*, one of the many

alleys of Leiden. Sonja pointed to a stencilled sign outside in Dutch and English warning that bikes parked against the wall would be thrown into the canal. 'I put that there,' she said proudly. There were no lace curtains to the living-room window, and on the sill were ornaments and Delft plates turned to the street for the benefit of passersby. We climbed into Sonja's high bed. We were light-headed and giggly, and at the same time apprehensive. 'I can't remember the last time... I'm, you know, out of practice. And, well, since you last saw me, I've acquired a scar. Emergency caesarean and all that. Thank you Lucas!' 'That's OK,' I said. 'Things that happen in the countryside.' I stroked her face. 'And besides,' I added, 'will I have lost the "*trucje*" you claim I had?'

She laughed and we kissed, and things were all right, they were good. I kept feeling I ought to say, 'Are we sure we know why we're doing this?' but for once I had the sense to keep my mouth shut and just enjoy it.

I woke in the night and couldn't get back to sleep. I lay there thinking about our first meeting in Paris. About how first impressions often prove wrong, but almost always have a kernel of truth. Sonja had appeared more robust and free-spirited, more anarchic and unconventional, than she turned out to be. She was all those things, but also more complicated and vulnerable than I'd realised: an untidy mix of things. Maybe we were all uneasy accommodations between contradictory aspects of ourselves. Wasn't it about time I learned to accept myself as a union of incompatibles – wasn't that the real *trucje*? A successful failure as a translator. A would-be lover whose nerve faltered at critical moments, or who made an approach only when he was sure it would fail. A sensitive reader of situations who often got things obtusely wrong. A bit of a mess, like everyone else.

Sonja stirred beside me, warm and enticing, and I snuggled up to her, began to stroke her softly until I felt her respond. Her caresses were different from those I'd remembered, as if she'd adapted to other lovers, learned a new language of touch, new rhythms. I felt a stab of jealousy, of sadness for all I'd foregone, for all the life she'd led without me.

The next morning, Sonja said, 'You grind your teeth in your sleep.'

'I know.'

'I don't remember you doing that in the old days. Or maybe I just slept better then.'

'No. It's one of those things that have come with age and experience.'

Her son Lucas arrived from Wassenaar. His friend's mother dropped him off and his friend waved through the car window as they drove away. At first I felt put out by his presence. But I watched Sonja and him together: comforting, easy, affectionate with each other. He was calm and self-contained and seemed good in his skin. He looked me up and down. 'So you're a friend of my mother?'

'Yes,' I said, 'a very old friend.'

'You're not that old,' he said.

Sonja and I laughed.

'Good,' said Lucas gravely, 'she needs friends.'

'We all do,' I said.

He smiled the smile of a boy who had friends to spare.

Sonja said that she'd read my English translation of *Malign Fragments*.

'Really?'

'I picked it up in Van Stockum, you know, looking for something hefty for a flight to Indonesia. Flicked through it, saw your name on the title page under the author's. I thought, hey, I know him!'

'And?'

'So I bought it. But I just couldn't get on with it, I'm afraid.'

'Fair enough, it's not for everybody.'

'So repulsive, that main character. Adolfo somebody... Him and his halitosis and his power trips. Why should we care?'

Lucas glanced up from the tablet in which he'd appeared to be engrossed and said, 'Mummy, what are you talking about?'

'Nothing darling, nothing important. Silly stuff.'

'Then why are you talking about it?'

'A very good question,' I said.

'Well, you know, *schatje*, sometimes even grown-ups do things for no good reason.'

'Sometimes? Often, you mean.'

Sonja and I laughed again and she touched my hand briefly, and Lucas caught the gesture and looked at me gravely, as if to say, *that's my mother you're toying with*. But she reached over and grabbed him and began to tickle him, smothering him with kisses until he was giggling and squirming away and crying out all at once. He tried to fend her off, his knees coming up to his chest. 'Stop, you're a bad mother, I'm going to get you back.'

And she was laughing and saying, 'I'll get you back if you get me back.'

'I'm reporting you.'

'Who to?'

'Social services and the police!' They both giggled.

And Sonja was right of course. Adolfo Tarir Espósito was a total *klootzak*. And so, most probably, was my revered author, Roberto Tunsch. Could *Malign Fragments* and I ever offer each other the mutual contentment I was seeing in front of me? Of course not. But then, I realised, that was the wrong question. Each was in its own sphere, and the challenge was to allow the two spheres to negotiate some kind of awkward, prickly coexistence in my psyche.

I exchanged mobile numbers with Sonja and we agreed we'd meet for coffee later in the day. I said my goodbyes. Lucas shook hands with me. Sonja kissed me quickly on the lips, and the boy looked anxiously from her to me, as if searching for clues.

I was hungry. So I bought rolls, sliced Gouda and some

tomatoes, and walked to the Galgewater. I sat on a bench facing the canal and ate a makeshift sandwich, listening to the gentle chug of the boats and the lapping of the water. On the far bank, half-a-dozen large old fishing vessels were moored in chevrons, converted into luxury homes. I had to fight off the shameless seagulls with my umbrella as the sun went in and out of dark clouds.

I sat for a long time, watching the sun grow large and darken, wondering whether something serious might come of this chance encounter, and how long it would endure. Was it my past with Sonja that I was reliving, or my future that I was shaping? Was it possible to translate episodes gone by into something that had new meaning? I was conscious of that familiar stiffness of the jaw, and I tensed and released the muscles.

At last, I stood. A seagull flapped up onto a rubbish bin close to me and began tugging at the debris of a takeaway meal. I had work to do in the archives. I turned and walked down a side street in the direction of the Hortus Botanicus, feeling buoyant, hopeful, apprehensive.

# Downhill

After I returned to London from Leiden, Sonja and I spoke most evenings on Skype for an hour or more, about little things, our day. The grainy image of her on the screen jumped jerkily from pose to pose. Did she see me that way, disjointed, out of synch? Without the touch or smell of her, it was a frustrating kind of intimacy. I wanted more. Or maybe less. After a few weeks, I was finding myself too unsettled to concentrate on my work.

One evening, Sonja said, 'I'm coming over next month.'

'To England? For a conference?'

'No, you idiot, to see you!'

'That's great,' I said, 'it's just...'

'You're turning fifty. Were you planning to ignore it?'

'I don't have that many friends.'

'I'm not surprised.'

'Ha.'

'But, hey, you're going to celebrate!'

She gave me her dates. 'Is it OK to bring Lucas, it's his autumn school break?'

'Yes, that would be lovely.'

I set about cleaning the flat, going through old papers stashed in cardboard boxes under the bed, drafts and notes, barely glancing at them before feeding them to the shredder. I even opened the box file containing my never-completed translation of Arguedas's novel, *El Sexto*. As I lifted out wads of paper, with their shrivelled and friable elastic bands, I caught sight of the first page of my draft, with the lines: 'By the light of the city's street lamps we could see the looming bulk of the prison in the distance...' I read on. There, on the first page, was the prison in all its gloom-inducing menace, with its foetid odour, darkened walkways, and the ominous clang of the steel gate behind the condemned men.

It was just bleak; it jarred with my now more buoyant

state of mind. I should have consigned it to the shredder, but I wavered. I returned the pages to the box file, and stashed it away in the shadows at the back of the filing cabinet, frightened to throw it out in case... In case what? I didn't know. Because I didn't like to leave something half-done, and still intended to finish it, hoping it would find its moment and be published? Because it marked a hard path travelled, over years? Because I needed it still, a dark, brooding counterweight to my more recent lightness?

As I was closing the drawer, I noticed a faded document wallet bearing the insignia of the Instituto Superior de Traducción e Interpretación de Lima, ISTI. The Institute. Beneath the logo was written in felt pen in my hand, '*Coursework – translations*'. I took out the folder and perched on the desk to look through it. It was as if I were sitting next to my younger self, enthusiastic, zealous, not quite as good as he thought he was.

There was a photocopy of Benedetti's short story, 'La noche de los feos', The Night of the Ugly, and, stapled to the back of it, my handwritten English draft done a quarter of century earlier as a class exercise. I read to myself the final paragraphs:

I could see nothing at all. But even so, I realised she now lay quite still, waiting. I cautiously stretched out my hand... My sense of touch transmitted a stimulating, powerful version of her. In the same fashion, her hands saw me.

At that instant I understood that I had to wrench myself (and wrench her) free of that lie that I had constructed... We were not that. We were not that.

My hand rose slowly to her face, it found the terrible sunken hollow and began a slow, convincing, convinced caress... Then, when I was least expecting it, her hand too reached for my face and began to move backwards and forwards over my scar...

I'd read the story a hundred times in Spanish, had tweaked my version endlessly. And now I was taken aback to be moved by the power of words on the page. I'd somehow managed to recreate in my clumsy translation, if only faintly, the emotional impact of Benedetti's original: two damaged people finding the courage to seek solace in each other. I told myself that getting older was no reason for sentimentality, and I turned the pages over.

On the back of the translation was a comment on my effort from the lecturer, in a scrawl I couldn't decipher, and below it, separately and in a rounded hand, this:

Very bad work Mister Chato Eengleeshman. Come and see me after the class. Signed, Señorita Gabi.'

There were two 'x's and a crude smiley face. Gabi – my fantasy woman, who'd kissed me in her car in Lima and invited me back to her place, the woman I lost from fear and a lack of self-belief – had written this, circa 1986, and I had no recollection of it at all. She must have been sitting in the same class as me when the lecturer handed back our translations, and I can only imagine she'd grabbed someone's red biro, maybe in the coffee break, and had scribbled on my coursework as it lay unattended.

I sat at my desk, trying to untangle the complex of thoughts and feelings, my obtuseness, my cowardice, opportunities missed, or not even seen. Where Gabi might be now, what she might be like. How I would have reacted, if I'd found this a year or two ago: I'd probably have set out on a quixotic quest to track her down. And if I had, what then? She'd no doubt be unlike I remembered her, but settled into middle age, mildly amused or irritated by my sudden reappearance. Nothing like the bright, intrepid, mysterious, terrifyingly attractive young woman of my memory. I came to the conclusion – a decade or two late, but still – that the whole Gabi thing was a chimera, a distraction. She, or rather the idea I had of her, was an impossible yardstick against which I judged the women in my life. No one (including the real Gabi) could measure up to an unfulfilled fantasy. Everyone else was bound to be inadequate, second-best.

I thought of Sonja, and felt an unfamiliar sense of ease and warmth, of anticipation. No doubt I'd start to worry about being tied down, about whether the feelings would last, about my limitations and hers, about our respective ugly scars. But that was part of my normal inadequacy. I just had to get on with it.

That night I had an anxiety dream. Prisoners marching in the sombre dark to an even more forbidding prison, dread, the clomp of boots in time with the thudding of my heartbeat. I awoke tense and ill at ease, with a niggling discomfort behind my breastbone. I'd had lamb curry for dinner, too salty, too spicy. I made a mental note to review my diet, and took a drink of water from the glass on the bedside table. It tasted bitter and metallic.

It was four in the morning. I couldn't get back to sleep. The discomfort grew worse, more acidic. I began to feel clammy and cold. Maybe not indigestion. A heart attack? My father had woken one morning with chest pains and was dead within the hour. Myocardial infarction, a coronary thrombosis. I knew these terms in four languages, but had no idea what they really meant, no sense of what might be happening in my body. I tried to breathe slowly and deeply, it could all be psychosomatic.

But the feeling at the back of my sternum was spreading and becoming an unambiguous, squeezing pain. I felt dog-tired. The pain grew stronger, became crushing, spreading up to my jaw and down my left arm. I had an anxious dread, a sense that I was standing on the edge of a precipice, knowing I had to jump; not an everyday anxiety about life, something more existential and terrifying.

I didn't want to be alone. An image of Sonja giggling on the sofa with Lucas flashed into my mind. I couldn't hold on to it, it darkened and faded. I wanted her to be with me, longed to hear her warm voice, ironic but sympathetic. Grimly, I imagined her arriving, my next planned visitor, in two weeks' time; ringing the doorbell, getting no response. Charming a neighbour into lending her the spare key, discovering my rotting corpse...

I told myself to get a grip. I tried to get up, sank to all fours, crawled to the bathroom, found an aspirin, chewed it. Not wanting the emergency services to find me naked, I wrapped a towel round my waist. I inched my way to the front door, and called 999.

\*\*\*

I lay in the hospital bed, trying to read on the tense, smiling faces of the nurses what my future held. My chest hurt. Had they pummelled me? Leads attached me to a monitor. I had a headache, and felt so weary I didn't know how to raise my head. I drifted back to sleep.

I had vivid dreams, maybe from the medication. I remember one where I was on top of a hill or mountain. It was rocky, with a stony path – precipitous – and at the top was a group of people. The sky was excessively blue, like in the old travel posters. The people were courteous in a professional way. At the very summit, they put me into a sort of open cart made of wicker. It was mounted on steel runners like a sled. They steered the contraption onto an iron track: I thought, *iron road, chemin de fer, ferrocarril, iarnród.* I knew it could not roll smoothly, 'as if on rails', as the French would say. It would grind and bounce over the bumpy track at precipitous speed. I could already hear the screech and squeal of iron on iron as the cart descended.

'What,' I asked, 'just me?'

'Don't worry, it is quite secure,' they said, 'and it is the only way down.'

They pushed me. I had a falling sensation that was frightening but also enthralling. I awoke, pleased to be alive but apprehensive about my new frailty.

The following day I felt a bit better. They came and inserted a catheter into my groin and some dye, and the medics watched on a screen as it wriggled its way up to my heart. It felt weird, as if a millipede was moving along inside me. The angiogram showed no lasting damage. They concluded that the episode had been mild – a warning or a dress rehearsal, not the real thing. They prescribed clot-busters, anti-clotting agents, plaque-settlers: it could happen again.

*\*\*\**

Towards the evening of my second day in hospital, Mark came to see me.

'How are you, old thing? I hear you've been in the wars.'

'Hello, Mark,' I said. 'It's good to see you.'

He gave me an awkward hug. I'd given his name as next of kin on the admission form. The hospital must have contacted him.

'My own stupid fault. An accident in waiting, what with the genetics, and not keeping fit, and so on. I think it was the shock of it more than anything.'

'Being mortal and all that.'

'I guess. Look, it's really good to see you.'

He sat on the bedside chair. 'We'll hit the squash court again when you're better.'

We'd played on and off for years, though not recently. He was better than me, but not as allergic to losing, so we were a fairly even match.

'The doctors say no explosive exercise. Steady as she goes.'

'Hate to break it to you, but your squash was never explosive.'

'Ha.'

I told him about Sonia. He remembered her name from my Paris days.

'Good for you. Delighted.'

'She comes with a seven-year-old.'

'Seven. Great. You've missed out the shitty bits. Literally.'

Then he told me his own news. 'Hey, you won't believe this, but I'm going to be a dad.'

'What!' I laughed. 'With Ana?'

'Yes, Ana and me, she's expecting.'

'Amazing.' I pressed his hand. 'How do you feel about it?'

'Over the moon, mate! Over the fucking moon!'

'Great. Congratulations.'

'Fathers!' cried Mark. 'Who'd have thought it, we're going to be fathers!'

'Yep,' I said, with only slightly exaggerated despondency, 'downhill all the way from here.'

'OK, so let's enjoy the ride!' He laughed loudly. A nurse came up and suggested, smiling but firm, that we keep our voices down and that I take it easy.

***

The effort to be cheerful had exhausted me, and once Mark had left, my sense of gloom returned. I debated whether to text Sonja and tell her to postpone her trip, or ask her to bring it forward if she could. I recalled the final passages of *Malign Fragments* where the hero Adolfo is dying of prostate cancer. His arms are spiked with lines, but he is still trying it on with the nurses. They smile at him, and offer to fetch his aged mother to sit with him; haughtily he refuses. Unlike Adolfo, I didn't care to be alone at the critical moment, should it come to that.

But it wasn't only the physical contact of another body I craved. It was the feeling that I shouldn't slip from the world unnoticed. I needed someone to bear witness to my existence, to the fact that I'd been here and would not be in the future. I rang Sonja's number.

A child's voice answered, in Dutch. 'Who is it?'

'Hello Lucas.'

'Hello.'

'You know I am?'

'Yes. You're the one who wrote that big book my mum has.'

'Yes, sort of. You looking forward to coming to England?'

'I don't know because I've never been.'

'Fair enough... Look, Lucas, is your mum there?'

There was a pause and Sonja came on the line. 'Hey, how goes it? How are things?'

It was so good to hear her voice, its engaging timbre, the note of friendly, mocking scepticism.

'Things could be better,' I said, and I poured out the story of my flagging heart.

'I'm coming straight over,' she said.

It felt like a reprieve.

## ACKNOWLEDGEMENTS

I am very grateful to several people for their help in the course of writing this novel: yet again to Alan Mahar for his fine editorial judgement, and Miles Larmour for his eagle-eyed scrutiny of the detail; to my colleagues and friends at Tindal Street Fiction Group for their critical support and encouragement over many years now; to four literary translators who generously took the time to talk to me at length about the nature of their art: Maureen Freely (who also invited me to an eye-opening lecture by a prominent theoretician and practitioner in the field), Susan Ridder, Chris Turner and Paul Vincent – they are in no way to blame for any remaining technical howlers; to translator Siân Miles for the enlightening chats on literary translation over the years; to my wife Didi Foster and sons Daniel and Joseph for the invaluable contribution of listening to the chapters read aloud; to Di Sinclair for useful insights for the final chapter; to Catherine Best for her meticulous copyediting; and last but not least to my calm, thoughtful and dedicated publisher at Holland Park Press, Bernadette Jansen op de Haar, and to her brother Arnold.

The work of several writers on the art and technique of translation was particularly useful for understanding the translator's mindset and for background, particularly David Bellos's *Is that a Fish in your Ear?* I also found helpful the writings of Umberto Eco, Kate Briggs, Maureen Freely and Tim Parks, as well as a textbook on translation, *Thinking Spanish Translation*, by Sándor Hervey, Ian Higgins and Louise Haywood.

People who know something of my personal history – that, for example, I've lived for periods in Lima and Paris – might be deceived into thinking this is an autobiographical novel. It isn't. The people and the relationships between them are fictional. This goes for the narrator as well; he is not a version of me. I have, however, taken isolated episodes of my life and used them out of context. So, yes, a computer translation programme I looked at in the 1980s actually did translate '*picos y bajos*' as 'pricks and bottoms', though my boss at the time was nothing like Claude Boutonnet. It's true that I was caught in an earthquake in Peru, though not in the 1980s. If a woman friend did once say to me, 'we seem to have got rather intimate', it certainly wasn't in Dutch. And while I did bite into a maggoty apple after a tour of the Lunahuaná vineyards, I'm not sure whether there really were two maggots or if by that point I was seeing double.

# The Author

Anthony Ferner was professor of international human resource management at De Montfort University and was head of research in the Faculty of Business and Law for twelve years. He retired in 2014. He has published many works of non-fiction, mainly about the behaviour of multinational companies.

His short story 'The Cat It Is That Dies' appeared in the anthology *The Sea In Birmingham*, edited by Gaynor Arnold and Julia Bell and published by Tindal Street Fiction Group in 2013. This story became the basis of his novella *Winegarden* published in 2015 by Holland Park Press.

Another of Anthony Ferner's short stories, 'The Tanks', was shortlisted for the *Irish Times* summer short story competition in 2014. His second novella, *Inside the Bone Box*, was published by Fairlight Books in 2018.

He has been a member of the Tindal Street Fiction Group, based in Birmingham, since 2010.

Holland Park Press is a unique publishing initiative. Its aim is to promote poetry and literary fiction, and discover new writers. It specialises in contemporary English fiction and poetry, and translations of Dutch classics. It also gives contemporary Dutch writers the opportunity to be published in Dutch and English.

To

Learn more about Anthony Ferner
Discover other interesting books
Read our unique Anglo-Dutch magazine
Find out how to submit your manuscript
Take part in one of our competitions

Visit www.hollandparkpress.co.uk

Bookshop: http://www.hollandparkpress.co.uk/books.php

Holland Park Press in the social media:

http://www.twitter.com/HollandParkPres
http://www.facebook.com/HollandParkPress
http://www.linkedin.com/company/holland-park-press
http://www.youtube.com/user/HollandParkPress